Grace Under Fire

A Camelot 2050 Anthology

David Cartwright

Printed by Ingramspark
First published in Great Britain in 2024 by David Cartwright

Printed and bound in Great Britain by Ingramspark
A catalogue record for this book is available from
The British Library
ISBN 978-1-0687133-0-9

David Cartwright was born in 1981, and raised in a Golden Age of Saturday morning cartoons. From that time and forever more he has been an avid watcher and reader of Science-Fiction and Fantasy, encompassing the likes of The Hitchhikers Guide to the Galaxy, The Walking Dead and the works of J.R.R. Tolkien and Neil Gaiman.

David has been a Jack of many trades, but so far, a master of none, working mostly in manufacturing whilst studying in Media and Counselling.

In 2017 he had finally had enough of the daily grind and quit the Nine to Five to become a fulltime author.

He lives in Hampshire, England with his family, cat and untameable moustache.

You can follow the author via his social media profiles;
D.Cart-writer on X
David Cart-writer on Facebook
D.Cart_writer on Instagram

Also by David Cartwright:

The Camelot 2050 Trilogy
Black Knight
Dragon Fire
Dark Magic

From LevelUp Publishing
Rendered Flesh

This book is dedicated to you, the readers who have propelled this journey, who have shown love and appreciation for the world of Camelot 2050, its characters, and its wonders.

Contents

Introduction

Story telling is something that has fascinated me for a long time. From bedtime stories read to me as a child to those first forays into independent reading and following the developing stories of episodic book, T.V. and film series.

From the Norse Sagas and the tales of Camelot to the latest science fiction extravaganza, tales of escapism and wonder have filled a large portion of my life-experience so, when in 2003, I started on the road that lead to the 2017 release of Camelot 2050: Black Knight, it felt like I was finally setting foot on a journey that would take me the rest of my life; becoming a writer.

Of course it was a steep learning curve. I had to develop a number of new skills and not all them linked to setting words on the page (unless you count editing, layout and type facing), but I also learned that, you're never 'finished'. The story gets to a point where it's 'good enough' but, excellent though it might be, you always notice little changes you can make, revisions and updates that come to you because, as you're writing, you're getting better, constantly developing.

Another thing I notice is there's never enough page space for everybody. Every character in a story has their fans and, as a writer, you ought to be a fan of all of yours. The problem with that is getting to spend enough time with all of them while keeping your story on track.

Which leads me to *Grace Under Fire*, the first Camelot 2050 Anthology. Within these pages are five stories dedicated to those characters who I wanted to spend more time with but just couldn't justify the page count.

More than that, it's a chance to expand the scope of the Camelot 2050 world, how it works, how it developed and where it is going to go in future.

I hope you enjoy reading it, as much as I enjoyed writing it.

David Cartwright
Author – *Camelot 2050*

<u>Tilt</u>

A light drizzle fell over the York tournament grounds, but the sun still shone through the sparse cloud. His Grace, Sir William Saxe-Coburg, the Duke of York, excused himself from his guest in the host's box and slipped out the entrance. Descending the back steps, he circled the public stands at a brisk pace and entered the arena by the participants' gate. The riggers were taking down the square fences of the sword arena and setting the field in preparation for a joust. At either end of the arena huge vid screens played scenes from the day's events in recap to keep the crowds entertained.

The Duke kept to the edge of the field and made his way to a small square marquis, decorated in the red and white of his house near the gate. Pulling back the canvas, he ducked inside. The page who was attending the tent's other inhabitant looked up, gulped and stood back at full attention until the Duke waved the young woman back to her task.

"Are you ready, squire?" he asked jauntily.

John Loxley, late of the Easingwold militia, now squire to the Duke of York, looked up from his arming stool and his expression was grim.

"Why are we doing this?" he grunted sullenly.

"For honour, glory and the entertainment of the people. You know, the usual," William replied wryly.

"It's a bloody farce is what it is," the squire shot back testily.

The Duke folded his long arms and regarded his 'squire' carefully. Most knights would select their trainees young, in their early teens, to begin the training. They would be taught the 'soft' skills and theory, educated in the ways of honour and knightly conduct as well as the standard curriculum, but John's case was wildly different.

Already in his late twenties, the broad-shouldered man before him had been raised to York's service for an act of great courage, an act that had seen him horrendously wounded in its execution. The great fire at Berkeley Castle had nearly claimed the life of Lord Berkeley's young daughter, but for the intervention of militiaman John Loxley of the Baronet of Easingwold's retinue. But, as was so often the way of such acts of heroism, the explosion of the castle's magazine had wrought a terrible cost on the valiant young man.

Sir William recalled the memory easily, since he had been there, and he was still astonished that Loxley had survived his injuries. He'd been more surprised at the time to learn that Baronet Easingwold hadn't the means for the extensive reconstruction procedures and had only intended, upon recognising John's heroism, to retire him on medical grounds. Such an end to his career was ill-fitting a veteran of actions in the Congo and the Far-East, so the House of York had intervened on John's behalf.

Fourteen months, a dozen reconstructive surgeries, an extended stint of physiotherapy and a new artificial arm later, and the newest squire to York was back on his feet. But he was no longer the cheerful, exemplary soldier his service record and psych profiles described.

He'd been stony-faced at his investiture, tight-lipped with his trauma counsellor, and barely engaged with the instructors for his theoretical lessons. But, in physical training and combat, a glimmer of the warrior he had been showed through, and so, William suspected, there was still hope.

"Squires don't joust," Loxley spoke evenly, dragging William's attention back to the here and now.

"There are precedents," the Duke shrugged, "and it's a simple exhibition, no grave matter of honour. In fact, it's a favour I'm doing Stafford."

John sucked his gunmetal-grey teeth irritably. "My gums itch," he complained sourly.

"Well, the doctor says the tissue has healed. There's no visible swelling and it's as likely to be a side-effect of anti-inflammatories as something that can be eased by them. Most likely it's psychosomatic," the Duke offered, not unkindly.

"You haven't answered my question, why are we doing this and who is this 'Geoffrey Mayland' kid anyway?"

Though his voice was sullen, William finally detected a trace of actual interest from John, so he indulged him.

"Stafford's latest squire, one Geoffrey Mayland, is a progeny. Skilled, smart and charismatic, but he tends to rest on his laurels and he's in danger of becoming not just complacent but arrogant too. Baron Dominic wants someone to 'knock him on his arse', in the Baron's own, well chosen words."

"Yeah? He's also, like sixteen, so why me, and why a joust of all things?" John was rising to the bait at last.

"Firstly," William raised a stern eyebrow. "He's seventeen and a half and-"

"Ah Christ! I've got ten years on the kid!" John protested.

"And," William went on, holding up a hand, "has already undergone his first round of augmentations, so don't feel you have to pull any punches. As for 'why you', it's all about reputation. You have one, as a hero no less. That kind of psychology plays a greater part than you might think. Also you're already a skilled combatant, and an unknown quantity as far as young Geoffrey is concerned. He has already proved himself amongst his contemporaries, so he really does need taking down a peg or two."

"But why a joust?" John held out his hands beseechingly. "Squires don't joust!"

"That's exactly why you will," William replied, a maddening, smug little smile playing on his lips. "You've both had only limited experience in simulated jousts, but this will be for real. It ought to level the field in a way no other contest could."

Squire Loxley hunched his shoulders. "I never asked to be a bloody hero," he spat vehemently, as if the word itself was distasteful.

"Maybe not, but don't underestimate the benefits of building a reputation early on." The knight smiled, "Anyway, if it makes you feel any better, once you do this you can take a step away from the spotlight for a while, okay?"

The arming tech held out John's tabard, emblazoned with the stylised branding based on the coat of arms of York, her intention to help the big squire into the garment. With a derisive grunt John stood, snatched the cloth away and draped it over his head, covering the ballistic cloth-lined carbon fibre breastplate that ought to protect him from the worst of the impending impacts.

Gesturing to the tech, William took the gorget to which his squire's shoulder guards would attach and stood in front of John to fit it. It seemed slightly odd to him that he was fitting armour to someone so close to his own stature, but he had an idea of what was troubling the squire, and it was his place to do all he could to help.

"You feel guilty, don't you?" William asked quietly, settling the armour plate and holding out his hand for the first pauldron.

"Why should I feel guilty?" John mumbled sourly.

"I've read your record; you lost comrades, friends, overseas in combat. You might have dealt with it at the time, considered it 'part of the job', but now? Now you have to deal with a completely different kind of consequence. Maybe you think you should have died in the explosion, maybe you feel that what you did wasn't so worthy of all this," the knight waved a hand vaguely to encompass the tent and indicate the stadium around them. "But, much as it's *for* you, it's not entirely *about* you."

"That doesn't make a lick of sense," John muttered.

William finished fitting the armour and placed his hands firmly on John's broad shoulders.

"You served, faithfully. I know it wasn't your choice after your father sold you into Easingwold's services, but you made the most of it. You might have served a household, but Camelot still owes you a debt for your service. Beyond that, Camelot holds true to its values and must be seen to do so. We could have simply pensioned you off, but why? When we could help you? When we could restore you after your injuries? You can always say 'no' but, I notice, you haven't. Yet," he finished with a slight wink.

John raised his gaze to meet William's. "What else can I do? All I know is how to fight."

"Anything, everything!" William chuckled. "You are beholden to no-one John, give the word and you're released from my service. You could go back to school or, with your record, you could go into policing or personal protection. Why, you could start a security company, I'd invest in you but, for the time being you need to heal and not here," the knight patted John's augmetic arm, "but here," and he tapped a finger to the squire's temple.

"The best way I can think of to do that is to stick to what you know."

John frowned a moment then reached a hand up to tug on his gorget, settling the armour more comfortably.

"Alright, I'll think about it." He held out a hand for his sword belt. "In the meantime, let's go whip this little Geoffrey bastard's arse."

"Honoured guests, welcome to the York showgrounds!" the announcer's voice boomed over the PA system. "At this time, the House of York is pleased to present an exhibition joust for your entertainment!"

William held the tent flap, awaiting John's cue.

"At the yellow flag, representing the House of Stafford, please give a warm round of applause for Geoffrey Mayland!"

John winced slightly at the thundering applause the crowd raised for his opponent. It wasn't a complete surprise, Stafford was a popular brand and those that wore its colours were always well received by the public.

"And, at the red flag, representing the House of York, it is our great pleasure to introduce, for his first appearance, John Loxley!"

William pulled the canvas aside and John stepped out into the grey light. The nearby audience clamoured and cameras flashed, but only when William revealed himself at his squire's shoulder did the noise begin to approach the level of Geoffrey's reception.

"Give them a wave!" William leaned in and growled solicitously from the corner of his mouth.

With a pained smile, John raised his arm, and again the volume rose.

"Not bad, not bad," William reassured his uncomfortable squire and led him toward the starting point. "I'd better get back to my box. Good luck, John," he smiled and held out a hand. John reached out and gave William the warriors' wrist-clasp handshake before the knight turned and left the field, waving to the crowd the whole time.

Taking a deep breath John turned and nodded to the attendants who managed his point. Two attended the weapons' rack where his lances and spare shield were hung. Two more stood by his bike holding his helmet and primary shield. Striding over, he grasped the handlebar of the latest incarnation Triumph Tiger which would serve as his mount for the joust. At one-hundred and eighty kilo's dry and with just over ninety foot-pounds of torque, the bike was capable of zero to sixty in just over eleven seconds. Its high-seated enduro styling was intended for cross-country and military use, but suited it toward jousting very well. It was a machine John was familiar with.

He cast a glance toward the big screen which was currently showing his opponent sat astride his own bike. John recognised a Norton Commando when he saw one, but the usual Cafe-Racer style had been tweaked, the suspension bumped high and off-road tyres fitted for this joust. Still, a clear sign of his opponent's inexperience, John chuckled to himself.

The Norton was a fine road-bike, capable of zero to sixty in fully half the time John's bike could achieve, but here on the woodchip and dirt floor of the arena, its lighter frame and lower torque would take a second or so to gain purchase, even with the knobbly off-road tyres.

John took a second to rev the growling engine, drawing the eyes of the audience and the cameras to his own position, a calculated move to annoy the poster-boy Mayland. Seating his helmet and offering his arm for the mag-lock shield, John took a breath and snapped his visor down. With the cheers from the stands and the noise of the arena finally muffled, John sighed in relief.

Holding out his hand, he received the offered lance and tightened his augmetic fingers around the shaft. Had his arm still been flesh it might have dipped to compensate for the added burden, but the bionic limb held firm and he felt the bike dip to the right as if it meant to fall. With a slight heave, John steadied himself and drew the lance into his body to centre the weight, holding it upright to signal 'at the ready'.

He watched the marshal signal his opponent and made out the raised lance signalling 'ready'. Turning toward John's point, the marshal raised a hand again and John lifted his lance, feeling all the while that, whether he was actually ready or not was of precious little importance right now.

The official nodded, satisfied and lowered the flag, again bearing the York crest, to signal the riders to be ready. John felt the sweat break out on his forehead and the slight nausea in his belly as he ground his titanium-alloy teeth in anticipation and twitched the throttle again.

The crowd hushed, awaiting the signal of the flag and the commencement of the bout. Seconds stretched out until, with a final glance to either end of the quarter mile stretch, the official raised the flag and the joust was on.

Both bikes roared and leapt forward, though John was slightly satisfied to see a tall spray of woodchip from the back of Mayland's machine as it sought purchase. The crowd roared in approval as, surging forward, John juggled the throttle and the lance, trying to catch the cradle bars protruding from his armour to bring the shaft to bear, frustrated by his own lack of finesse. Much as he'd practised in the VR sims, they were based on the assumption a Knight would be astride one of Camelot's synthetic C.T.E.E.D.'s.

The A.I. driven Cybernetic Transport Engagement and Evasion Devices were styled after horses and fully capable of guiding themselves toward a target, leaving the knight free to wield their weapons; the motorcycle beneath him now, not so much.

In apparent disdain of his own fumblings, his opponent seemed all too comfortable in the saddle, his lance dropping smoothly into position as the two raced toward one another for the clash.

The distance decreasing and the speed ever increasing, John, grimacing with the effort, managed to seat his lance and bring it to bear at the last second as he braced for impact.

Looks could be deceiving and, as John's wobbling lance glanced off his opponent's shield, Geoffrey's lance likewise slipped on John's midriff armour and dragged across the plates. Geoffrey struggled to retain the weapon as it swung, bouncing off the tilt rail, unbroken.

The riders steadied their machines and carried the ungainly shafts to the far ends of the course. Turning, they each rode to their starting points as the crowd cheered and jeered in equal measure.

John furrowed his brow in frustration, some of it spared for the crowd but most reserved for himself. If only he'd managed to break his lance he'd be one up but, as his old C.O. would say, 'Ifs and buts don't win wars'.

The official jogged out and dropped the flag again to let the riders commence the charge.

This time, John was more prepared for the struggle between bike and lance, and managed to gun the engine and hold the weapon in position for the strike.

The dulled carbon tips impacted their targets and shattered with a resounding 'Crack!' as they were designed to do. John 'whuffed' as the shock of his strike ran from his arm into his shoulder and, at the same moment, the impact of Mayland's lance on his shield threatened to tip him off his bike.

They passed so quickly that he didn't see how well he'd struck. The front wheel of his bike wobbled skittishly and John had to drop his shattered shaft as he grabbed the handlebars with both hands and fought to stay upright, until his feet kicked out from the pegs for balance. With a sigh of relief, he brought the bike under control and turned smoothly at Geoffrey's end of the run to ride back to his own starting position, kicking up a spray of chips of his own.

As he passed the judges' box on his return, he saw the score screens flash up the numerals. Both squires had struck, both knights had scored. He had two more lances left to change that.

His lance arm, his prosthetic, felt neither the worse nor better for the strain, but his shoulder and chest on the left, his shield arm, were throbbing slightly from the strike. He pulled up and dropped the bike into neutral, stretching and flexing the pulsing muscles, rolling his shoulder before taking grip of the handlebar once more and signalling for a new lance.

The Mayland kid was good. He'd brought his lance into position smoothly and hit John like a truck. Glancing up at the screen, he saw the replay and winced as he watched himself jerk in the saddle but stay upright. The camera switched to show Mayland, and Loxley was gratified to see his opponent in similar straits, reeling back from John's own blow, the bike rearing with the force. But Geoffrey recovered his balance and control with almost miraculous speed, riding the wheelie to the end of the tilt to the delight of the crowd.

The kid was good, John could give him that.

Lance in hand, he tried to come up with some plan, some tactic to overcome the young showboat but, with his limited experience of the joust, all John could think of was 'hit him harder'.

He turned his helmed head toward Sir William, seated in the York stand. Straining his eyes, he just saw the knight give him a small nod and a smile.

'A good enough start then,' John thought and blew out a shallow breath.

The competitors back at their stations, the official lowered the flag again and signalled for readiness. Both riders raised their lances, the flag flew upward and the engines howled again, higher and louder this time as they left their marks, the crowd cheering along at the spectacle.

Finding his cradle with more surety, John tried to pick a decisive spot to strike, one that would unseat his opponent and give him a clear advantage. The bout wouldn't be over until three lances were broken or one competitor was forced to yield, but with a scoring lead and his opponent on foot, Loxley would have a clear advantage.

He quickly ran his tongue over his teeth as the two bikes raced toward one another, so intent on picking his point of strike that he took his eyes off the tip of Mayland's lance.

It happened in the blink of an eye. John raised the tip of his lance to catch the younger squire high in the chest, but apparently Mayland had seen that coming and had the augmented reflexes to deal with it. His shoulder dropped and John's lance glanced off unbroken, while Geoffrey's lance hit Loxley low-centre in the chest, carrying him from his saddle as the bike sped away without him.

John hit the ground before he could really make out what was happening, but the thud of impact and his ungainly roll through the dirt were clear indicators.

Shaking off a moment of dizziness, John cursed vehemently and pushed himself back to his feet. His chest was throbbing and his lungs heaved to catch his breath. His shield was gone, the mag-lock had cut out to stop it injuring him in his fall. His sword was at his hip, but he was as unfamiliar with that as he was the joust. The crowd was on its feet, frothing at this new twist to the event.

Mayland reached the York end of the tilt, and the tension in the air took on an electric crackle of anticipation. A knight unseated from their mount could fight on, on foot. Each house's weapon stand held one lance ready for their opponent for just such an event. The tilt would continue until a third lance was broken or a knight (or squire in this case) was forced to yield.

Teeth clenched, chest heaving and sweat pouring from his brow, John stood in his lane. Rage and frustration at himself and the snot-nosed, silver-spoon fed little oik sitting so serenely on his bike churned in his gut. He wanted to kill the little bastard, wanted him to hurt, wanted to watch him squirm before he died but, as he watched, the yellow-armoured squire hesitated and turned his head, lance in hand, to confer with John's own crew.

In a flash of realisation that cut through the haze of fury that was building, John remembered where he was and what he was doing. Mayland wasn't riding because he wasn't sure what was going on, because he was just a kid, and this was just a game. John blinked as he remembered, he was supposed to either draw his sword and indicate 'ready', or drop it to the floor to signal his surrender. He had not yet drawn the weapon, and so, Mayland wouldn't ride.

Taking a deep, shuddering breath and shaking his head to clear it, John reined in his spiralling anger and grinned to himself. This gave him a chance, albeit a slim one.

He raised his head to watch until he was sure he had Mayland's attention. The crowd hushed, curiosity overcoming their enthusiasm.

Slowly, John raised his hand and made a beckoning gesture with his fingers.

The crowd went mad. Mayland turned toward the York staffer and spoke urgently. The staffer simply shrugged and stepped away. If Mayland refused to ride he would forfeit. If he rode down an unarmed squire he'd suffer some repercussions, maybe a reprimand, but John had signalled it, essentially taking the responsibility on himself.

With a slight twitch of his head, Mayland raised the new lance and rode. This time straight toward John, no tilt bar to separate them, the younger squire simply rode down on his opponent, lance dipped to strike.

The crowd's cheering faded from John's perception as he watched the Stafford rider race toward him with singular intensity. Blocking all distractions from his mind he watched the Norton come on, trying to gauge its speed and watching the lance tip as it danced with the vibrations of the bike. Mayland held the lance and his elbow high, clear of his midriff and braced to strike down as he aimed it toward John's chest.

John shifted one foot slowly back to brace himself, bent his knees to lower his centre of balance just a little and brought up his fists in a boxer's stance.

That threw Mayland. John could almost feel the youth's confusion as his opponent bobbed gently on the balls of his feet. Still, the bike came on and the crowd held its collective breath.

As Mayland's lance came toward him, John weaved, rolling back on his bracing leg and twisting his body away. The lance tip sailed past him and he thrust forward with all his strength, swinging his outstretched augmetic forward as hard as he could and clothes-lining the youth as he passed.

The sheer force of impact made him gasp as the linkages between his prosthetic and his bones and muscles protested the abuse, but he carried Mayland clear off the back of the Norton, arms and legs outstretched, lance and shield flying free, and threw the slight figure to the ground.

The stands fell silent. Using his natural arm, John gripped the augmetic as it hung limp, and rolled the rebuilt shoulder just to make sure it was up to what he had planned next. He gave the stressed prosthetic a shake out before reaching down to grip his opponent. Despite William's assurances, the stricken squire seemed much smaller than John had expected. His big alloy fingers closing around the gorget and the top of his opponent's breastplate, John hoisted the dazed youth into the air.

Loxley prized Mayland's faceplate from his helmet and brought the handsome young man in close.

"Yield," John grunted simply.

Head lolling and eyes blinking, the Stafford squire raised his hand in surrender.

"I yield," he announced muzzily and John lowered him gently to the ground.

The stands exploded as the judges struck Mayland's score, and the big screen zoomed in on John who turned and, glad that his helm was hiding his sheepish expression, gave them a hesitant wave.

Geoffrey was raising himself to his elbows, so John offered him a hand as the medics rushed toward them.

The P.A. rang out. "Assembled guests, York gives you your victor. John Loxley of York!"

On his feet, Geoffrey held John's hand high for the furiously cheering crowd before pulling the broad squire down.

"That was awesome!" Geoffrey yelled into John's ear, beaming like a child who'd just made their first stage appearance for their parents to watch.

The pure, sincere and unabashed joy of his 'defeated' opponent's expression triggered a spark in John's overwhelmed brain and he reached up to unclasp his helmet, lifting it from his sweat-streaked brow.

"John Loxley," he stated simply, offering his hand.

"Geoffrey Mayland," the younger squire shot back, taking the offered hand and shaking it vigorously, "but my friends call me 'Swift'!"

The medics reached them then, and each squire was led back to their own pavilion for a preliminary medical assessment.

William entered the pavilion as a tech was doing final checks and repairs to John's abused augmetic. The big squire's ribs had been tightly bound by the medics, but a purple bruise was already creeping out from under the clean white bindings.

"That was phenomenal, John," he congratulated the squire. "Well done. I must say you exceeded my expectations, well done."

"Thank you my liege," John replied, honestly grateful for the knight's words.

"In fact, someone would like to come in and see you, if you'll allow."

"Who?" John was puzzled. Which news outlet could possibly have the clout, or the interest in seeing him so shortly after the bout?

"Your opponent, Geoffrey," William grinned.

John blinked, momentarily taken aback.

"Alright," he conceded.

Still grinning, William pulled back the tent canvas and a slight, fair-haired young man in a neck-brace, sling and yellow Stafford tabard, entered the pavilion fairly buzzing with excited energy.

"That was amazing!" he announced without a moment's preamble. "The way you took me off that bike? Absolutely amazing, I'm going to be sore for weeks!"

"Surprised you're not now, jumpin' around like that." The sheer exuberance of this strange meeting had John completely off-guard, but Geoff simply waved the concern away.

"Oh not now, too many painkillers for that," he winked and, as if just remembering himself and his station, he took a deep calming breath and blew it out slowly, beaming mischievously the whole time.

Turning slightly, he addressed, somewhat more formally, Sir William.

"My lord, might I congratulate you upon your squire's victory. I have never seen such bull-headed stubbornness."

"It's hardly my doing, Geoffrey. His tactics went against practically everything I've tried to teach him," William smirked. "But, stubborn as he is, he refused to die after the Berkeley Castle fire and refused to be bested by one as gifted as yourself, so, in this instance, I think we might count his Ox-like demeanour as a virtue."

Geoffrey's eyes widened in surprise and sudden realisation as he turned to address John himself. "Berkeley Castle? Of course!"

"You didn't know?" John asked, surprised by Geoffrey's ignorance.

Geoff shrugged in exaggerated embarrassment. "Let's say I forgot, because that sounds better than admitting I was lax on my pre-bout research."

William held up a hand for their attention. "Excuse me for a minute, I've things to attend to. Once again, congratulations John."

He left, beckoning the almost forgotten tech to follow.

John returned his attention from the departed knight to the still grinning youth.

"So that's how you did it then?" he gestured smugly toward John's augmetic. "That's how you clothes-lined me off a speeding motorcycle like swatting a fly?"

"Would you have expected it, even if you had done your pre-bout research?" the big squire's curiosity was getting the better of him.

"To be totally honest? No, no I wouldn't. No-one's ever done anything like that before. Knights get dragged off sometimes, but that? That was one for the history books."

John grinned slightly. "Let that be a lesson then, even the most thorough research can't tell you when someone's about to do something bloody stupid."

"You say 'stupid', I say 'inspired'." The younger squire got a thoughtful look about him.

"I hope you won't take this the wrong way," he began cautiously, "but, as someone who uses self-deprecation on a routine basis, I can't help but feel you were being serious there?"

John shrugged, wincing at the discomfort the motion brought. "Maybe, what of it?"

"Well, for someone who just made a squire's exhibition bout the talk of the town, I'd assume you'd be pretty happy about that." The Stafford squire looked suddenly pensive, as if he was afraid to open a line of questioning that might anger the bigger man.

John interlaced his fingers and leaned forward, resting his elbows on his knees with a deep sigh.

"You wouldn't understand," he stated simply.

"Maybe I wouldn't, but I can try," Geoffrey smiled encouragingly.

As John finished recounting the story of his service, Geoffrey listened with growing awe.

"So," the younger squire said at last, "You've seen some—"

"—If you say 'real shit' I'll deck you all over again." John grunted. "This ain't a bloody movie."

"... things." Geoff finished apprehensively.

"Yeah," the older squire shrugged, "You could say that I have."

"And yet you still don't think you deserve this?"

"Maybe I don't, who's to say?"

Geoffrey shrugged, "Well, I'd say you do. Maybe more than any of us."

"What does that mean?" John frowned up at the open and honest young man.

"Look John, I can't really comment on PTSD or survivor's guilt, but what I can empathise with is imposter syndrome. You, at the very least, have already displayed selflessness, courage and the willingness to fight to liberate others from oppression. You're proven, John, what did I ever prove? That a young man from a wealthy and privileged background can be a talented athlete and media darling, that's what. Should Camelot ever call on me I have no idea what I'll do, fight, run or hide but, with someone like you alongside me I know it'll be harder for me to be a coward."

"You really mean that, don't you?" John asked, a small smile playing at the corner of his mouth.

Geoffrey blushed, just slightly, "I do. Now come on you stubborn ox, there's a post tournament party to get ready for."

"Hmm," John inclined his head thoughtfully, "'Ox', I like that."

Outside a deep voice bellowed in frustration, "Where is that blasted boy? I'll have 'is hide if he doesn't show up soon."

"Oh balls," Geoff wailed, "I lost track of time, Sir Dominic is going to kill me!"

"Don't you worry, Swift," John declared in good-humour. "I'll talk to 'im, it's my fault you're late, so it's the least the Ox of York can do for ya!"

Taking Geoff firmly by the shoulder they stepped out to face the Baron of Stafford's ire, together.

Covert

Engine purring, the Lamborghini traced the evening roads of Istanbul. The golden sunlight of the late spring evening cast cool shadows across the city streets between the tall modern buildings as the luxury sports car wove along the busy roads. Glass and steel shimmered, interspersed with red tiled roofs and the deep greens of the city parks, all alongside the intricate plaster patterns and rich colours of the scattered Mosque spires.

Leaving the city and sliding easily through the domestic traffic outside Demirci, the driver opened the throttle under the azure sky as they headed for the Yavuz Sultan Selim Bridge. The evening sun glittered on the water below and the sports car howled in joy at being given its head. Leaving the main roads behind, the driver took a road headed for the coast near Iriva as the setting sun finally kissed the horizon behind them.

The soft sound of tyres on asphalt became the harsh crackle of gravel as the car swung off the road and through the wrought iron gates of a walled estate. It joined a short queue of similar luxury vehicles waiting in the circular drive for the uniformed valets to take the cars for parking, whilst an ornamental marble fountain sent sparkling cascades of water into the air, underlit by shifting colour lamps. A soft breeze stirred the branches of the Turkish oaks and fig trees that lined the drive, but the wind was warm and smelled of spices and seawater.

The house at the end of the drive was impressive but not as sprawling as many of the old manors of Europe. The Ottomans liked to impress but they didn't tend to entertain the sheer extravagances of the old European nobility. Three stories of pale cream plaster with high ceilings and large, multi paned windows looked out toward the green lawn and gate. To the East, a short way across the gravel was the garage (joined by a subterranean tunnel for security according to the building plans) and to the West, close to the manor, was a private hammam, or bathhouse. An impressive setup, but not overly ostentatious.

Mother Superior Bethane Sciarra, Commander in the Holy Templar Order and agent of the Vatican, let the simple thrill of the drive ease out of her and mentally reviewed the mission dossier in her head. If the rumours were true (and the Vatican Security Council had gone to great lengths to verify them) the Ottoman Intelligence Agency had pulled off a serious coup as far as the wider security community was concerned.

They'd supposedly pulled intel out of Russia.

That vast country had been an intelligence black hole for centuries. Oh, agents went in, occasionally, a few reports came out, but never much of substance and they soon dried up. None of the agents ever returned. But somehow, if the rumour was true, the OIA had a report of significant value and, like any agency worthy of the name, they had done all they could to keep it to themselves.

But word *had* leaked.

Of course they'd denied it. Any mention of it and they clammed up immediately. The Ottomans weren't an enemy, but they weren't exactly 'friends' either and, if Bethane had to guess, they were holding the information as future leverage in some high stakes diplomatic discussion. The agency who managed to get a copy for themselves was going to gain themselves some serious kudos in the community, and the VSC intended to be that agency.

The politics aside, Bethane's mission was to gain access to and copy the data. An in-and-out job, minimal 'contact' (in the sense of out and out violence in any case), which was why she was attending a party. The house owner and host for tonight, one Ekrem Macit Kartal, was outwardly known as a developer and successful architect. Unknown to him (hopefully anyway, as far as Bethane was concerned) the Vatican had cracked his cover as an operative and handler for the OIA, and the initial recipient of the report she needed. Using an established cover as a representative of an investor company, Bethane would use the cover of the party to gain entry to the house, then infiltrate Ekrem's office (second floor, Northwest corner) and his computer to copy the drive.

Bethane had argued for a simple night-insertion, a stealth op to gain entry, but the Deacons of the VSC, especially Deacon Aurelia, had opted for using the cover of the party. Kartal was celebrating winning a sizeable contract, so instead of just their charge and his immediate staff, the twelve security guards that patrolled the house and grounds would have to watch over Kartal, his three hundred guests and sixty servers, cooks and entertainers. Of course there would be thirty of them instead of just twelve, but the Deacons thought the ratio would allow for an easier operation. That meant a detailed cover story and at least an hour of mindless conversation with other investors.

Not that Bethane didn't have support of her own. Her operations' coordinator had hacked into the house's security feeds. Two agents were on station outside the gates (far enough away as to avoid suspicion but close enough to respond if required) and another two held position just offshore in a dinghy for the same reason. They even had a plant in the security detail for the night. Bethane briefly considered the movies she'd seen where a dashing agent would walk into such a situation alone and shook her head with suppressed mirth.

The car in front of her moved and she pulled up to the valet station.

"VT Control," she spoke quietly, her implanted throat mic picking up the words and sending them to her operations officer. "Confirm surveillance access, over."

"Control confirms VT Alpha," the steady voice of her operational support officer fed back. "Got you on the villa cameras, no problems."

A young man opened the door for her and, reaching for her clutch purse, she stepped out of the low car's driver seat. At least she didn't have to worry about swanning around in some ridiculous cocktail dress. Out of respect for her hosts' beliefs she wore a modest but flatteringly cut suit jacket with loose cullote pants in copper satin, and a full headscarf in patterned marina blue. The headscarf covered her military grade comms unit but that was disguised as a commercial hands-free earpiece for just such an operation. It also covered her close-cropped hair which was rather more distinct, and Bethane was thankful. She hated wearing wigs on these kinds of ops.

Bethane smiled her thanks to the valet and strolled up the steps to the manor door, taking note of the security guards on either side. Pale grey suits, expensive and well cut, couldn't quite hide the slight bulge of shoulder holsters on each guard. She suppressed a grimace. She'd known they would be armed but it didn't make her feel better about her own lack of weaponry. There was a metal detector discretely framing the door but the team had anticipated its presence, so she wasn't carrying anything overtly offensive or that contained more that a small trace of metal. Presenting her clutch to the guard for a cursory inspection she stepped through the detector and waited a moment before the guard gave a brief nod and handed it back to her.

"VT Control, this is VT Alpha. I'm in." she spoke softly and stepped into the main hall, smiling as she accepted a champagne flute from a proffered tray as she passed. The hall was tall, wide and brightly lit, no convenient shadows or heavy curtains to hide behind. The twin staircases up to the second floor were especially open, no concealment opportunities at all there. But that wasn't the goal right now. Once all the guests had arrived, they, and the servers, ought to move out into the gardens where the main party was occurring and that would be her window.

Bethane swept her gaze around the hall, then passed between the curving stairs and out the back of the mansion into the gardens. The oncoming night was darkening the sky but the emerging stars had been supplemented by soft strings of lights over the pristine green garden. The hubbub of quiet conversations was backed by a string quartet and grand piano accompaniment, the musicians stationed on a low stage just off to Bethane's left. Running the length of the lawn, a series of long pavilions housed a bar, buffet and even a small crew of chefs labouring over hot plates, searing fish and vegetables, preparing lahmacun or rolled dolma fresh for the guests.

Stepping down into the crowd she addressed her com, "VT Control, this is VT Alpha starting perimeter assessment.

"Got you VT Alpha," the calm voice of her controller came back, "Following you on cams."

Bethane worked her way around the edge of the assembled guests trying to get a feel for any potential threats to the mission. It wouldn't be the first time she'd stumbled across fellow operators with the same objective or, more commonly, the direct opposite intent. She was at the far end of the garden from the house when her earpiece chirruped.

"VT Alpha, we *might* have a problem."

"Where?" Bethane kept her voice low as she smiled to a well dressed diplomat who'd raised a glass in her direction.

"Just coming to the top of the back steps now, take a look." the controller instructed.

Turning her head that way, Bethane had cause to pause in her sweep. The man at the top of the steps was head and shoulders taller than anyone else in attendance. His white hair cascaded down an immaculate charcoal grey suit which bore a coloured flash on the breast.

Bethane recognised him from a dossier she'd read some time ago, one that should have had no bearing on the current mission. Sir Jerome Grayson, Knight of the Round Table and Duke of Oxford adjusted a crisp white shirt cuff and descended the steps to the grass with all the predatory grace of a tiger.

"What in God's name is he doing here?" Bethane sighed, expertly maintaining her smile despite her feelings.

"He's a late addition to the guest list, that's for sure," Control sounded tense. "Might be here to invest himself. How do you want to proceed, Actual? Scrub the mission or go ahead as planned?"

Bethane only hesitated a moment.

"We proceed, once this intel gets to their central office we'll have no chance of laying our hands on it."

"Then we better do it quickly. As a senior knight, there's a chance he's aware of your status beyond an officer of the Templar Guard, do not engage him at all."

"I'll do my best, Control." Bethane replied uncertainly.

For all her training and experience, the Knight of the Round Table was a genetically enhanced and bionically augmented super-soldier (although, beyond his seven-foot plus height and apparent albinism you'd hardly notice any obvious augmentations). Jerome's 'gifts', built into him by the Cult of Merlin, put her at a distinct disadvantage and, as was the nature of such covert intelligence, it was likely far from complete. God alone knew what specific abilities the Duke had within reach of a mere whim, whilst hers were largely at her fingertips. A distinct disadvantage from where Bethane sat. No, she'd have to try and avoid all contact if possible. The only way to win *this* facet of the game was not to play.

Surreptitiously keeping an eye on the Knight, not so difficult given his height, Bethane moved to the farthest end of the immaculate lawn, lifting a fluted glass from a passing server, and joined a knot of guests in casual conversation.

Whenever Jerome moved closer, Bethane made some brief excuse and moved to a new group, orbiting the party, keeping as much distance as she could between them.

This dance led Bethane back to the stairs of the patio that backed onto the house but, as she turned to move once more a smiling man neatly intercepted her.

"Good evening," Ekrem Kartal smiled pleasantly at her, holding out a hand in greeting. "Welcome to my party, I hope you are finding everything to your liking?"

Bethane immediately adopted her cover persona. Inclining her head with a demure smile of her own she took the offered hand and his lips brushed the back of her hand lightly. Bethane groaned inwardly, she'd have preferred a firm handshake herself, but the action gave her a little insight as to who she *might* be dealing with.

"Very much so, Mr Kartal." she replied brightly, masking her thoughts behind her cover.

"Please, all my investors can call me Ekrem, though I do not know your name?"

"Marchesi, Vittoria Marchesi," Bethane answered easily. "I'm here representing Toscani Holdings."

"Ah yes," Ekrem smiled broadly. "Your investment was most timely. The entire project might have fallen through but for your intervention."

"We like to think we know a good opportunity when we see one."

"Well, maybe you can help me convince this gentleman of the benefits of ongoing investment in the development?" he gestured over her shoulder and, as Bethane turned she realised too late that she'd been trapped.

Jerome loomed over her shoulder. His approach had gone completely unnoticed by the Vatican agent.

"Oh, I'm not sure there's much I could do to sway a Knight of Camelot," she affected the air of someone totally intimidated by the sheer presence of Jerome, lowered her gaze and tried to present herself as beneath the arrogant noble's notice. Inwardly she cursed. Maybe Jerome had noticed her avoiding him and she'd sparked his interest herself, perhaps it was an ambush. Either way she'd just have to play it out.

"I'd rather keep our business between ourselves Ekrem," the Knight's voice was smooth, cool and only slightly aloof. "And why spoil a pleasant evening with business? There are other matters to discuss, would you excuse us m'lady?"

With barely a glance at her, Jerome dismissed Bethane and she gratefully took the opening to slip quickly up onto the patio and away from the conversation.

"That was a close one," Control whispered in her ear.

"You're telling me," Bethane mumbled, "*Dio santo*, that was close."

"You know that if I put that in my report the Deacons will haul you in for a disciplinary," the quiet voice chided her.

"My cover's intact, they haven't made me, yet," Bethane reassured them in return.

"Not the close call, the blasphemy," there was a smug tone in the reply.

Bethane rolled her eyes.

"Let's just get on with this," she grimaced.

"Alright, all the guests are in and our embedded agent is on station at the foot of the landing stairs. You're good to go."

"Keep an eye on Kartal and Grayson, I want to know where they are at all times."

With that Bethane eased her way back into the house and walked quickly across the floor toward the security guard who should be their in-house contact.

"Oderint dum metuant," Bethane spoke quietly.

The guard glanced around the room, now notably devoid of guests and staff.

"Timor potens est motivum," he answered smoothly and stepped aside.

The call and response phrases offered and accepted, Bethane made her way quietly and quickly up the sweeping stairs and along the landing to the second set, taking her out of sight of the main hall. Creeping across the lush carpet of the dark corridor, she made her way to the Northwest corner and Kartel's office.

Reaching under her blouse, she pulled a connection lead, carefully weighted and calibrated not to set off the metal detector, out from around her waist. Plugging a fine jack into her earpiece she drew a nondescript security swipe card out of her clutch and fed the micro-USB plug into the magnetic strip.

"Control, ready?" she queried.

"The code scrambler is go, swipe now," the instruction came back crisply.

Drawing the card through the door reader, Bethane held her breath as the light flickered and then turned green.

Opening the door gently, the Vatican operative moved inside like a shadow, relying solely on the ambient moonlight and the secondary glow from the exterior lighting to guide her way to the desk and its integrated computer. Stowing the card and wrapping the lead around her wrist Bethane took her 'Smartphone' from her clutch. She turned the device on and placed it on the polished glass touchpad surface before activating the computer. As the display started to glow Bethane turned to close the room's curtains, in case the light gave her away.

A holo-screen projected and an icon span as she waited patiently. The security screen displayed a small black box in the corner, and lines of code started writing themselves across it.

"How's it going, Control?" Bethane commed. She wasn't even doing the hack.

Her 'phone' was actually a cleverly disguised modem allowing her support agent to work a little computerised magic from the apartment that served as their base of operations back in the city.

"Working on the security, shouldn't take long." the voice in her ear reassured her calmly.

"What's the status on Kartal and Jerome?"

"Look out the window." Control replied, a hint of irritation in the voice.

"Come on control," Bethane chided.

"Still together, still talking. Moving to the far end of the lawn."

"Good, now let's get the data and get out."

"Working on it."

Bethane sat and listened for any telltale sounds from the corridor outside whilst the screen crawled with code.

"We're in." Control alerted her. If there were going to be any problems they would come soon. Anyone working on sensitive or confidential information *might* have an app set up to tell them when their computer was active just as a precaution, but Bethane was sure her operative could handle such things.

"No outgoing signals, searching for access restricted files."

This was the bit Bethane had been dreading. The hack was out of her hands, nothing for her to do but wait. Not that she wasn't trained for it, but the tension of waiting always made her restless. Moving to the window she twitched the curtain carefully.

Down below she quickly picked out Jerome walking with Kartal toward the hammam, away from the party and, apparently, unregarded by the OIA operative's domestic security.

Something nagged at her, so she let the curtain drop and went to the westward window to keep track. Kartal was walking stiffly and Jerome was *very* close to his host. She lost sight of them as they entered the bathhouse.

"Control?" she queried softly.

"Just cracking the codes for these encrypted files, twenty seconds," Control responded.

"Great, I've just seen Grayson taking Kartal into the hammam and I think Kartal was under duress. Are there any cameras in there?"

"A couple, why?"

"Because I want to know what's going on."

"I'm kind of in the middle of things right here, VT Alpha."

"Dammit, Control, just check the cameras'!" Bethane ordered firmly.

"There's no-one in there," Control reported.

"Yes there is, I saw them go in," Bethane urged and then realisation dawned. "Someone else is in the system, they're covering Jerome's tracks."

"Alright just gimme a sec," the hurried tapping of keys came over the link as Bethane waited. "Alright, oh Jesus Mary mother of Christ!"

The outburst caught Bethane off guard.

"What, Control, what's happening?"

"Grayson has Kartal up against the wall, his hand is... in him!"

"What? Say again Control?"

"Grayson's hand is in Kartal's stomach, there's blood everywhere! Kartal seems to be talking though."

"Okay, what's the status of the hack?" Bethane could hear the tremor in the operative's voice.

"Erm, I'm past the security, just verifying that the intel is here,"

"Stay on it, I'll keep an eye out."

Bethane's mind raced. Aside from the fact that his actions were completely at odds with Camelot's values, and given that someone was erasing his presence from the security feed, if Jerome was interrogating Kartal so brutally there could only be one reason for it. He was here for the same intelligence she was. As if summoned by that thought, the knight stepped into view below, wiping his bloodied hand on a towel. His eyes turned upward to the window. Swearing to herself, Bethane dropped the curtain.

"He's coming, get the data!"

"Alright, uploading to the device storage now, twenty seconds."

Moving to the table, the Vatican operative pulled her scarf up over her nose and stood with her hand hovering over the device, ready to cut and run as soon as the transfer was complete. She knew it would be close. If he simply rushed the guard Jerome would be at the door within that small window of time, so she quickly ran through alternative escape routes.

"Done!" Control announced and Bethane snatched up the device and went back to the window just as the door burst inward, dragging much of the reinforced frame with it. The towering Duke of Oxford stood outlined in the faint light of the corridor.

Wrenching the window up Bethane swung her legs over the sill and kicked off, dropping to the ground where she landed like a paratrooper, ankles together, knees folding and rolling to disperse the impact. Coming swiftly to her feet, she dropped the data storage device into her clutch and dashed towards the front courtyard. There were shouts from the other side of the house and a guard came around the corner toward her, weapon drawn.

Holding her hands defensively in front of her Bethane drew the wire from her wrist and, as the guard came forward issuing challenges she stepped smoothly into him. Wrapping the lead around his wrist she took control of the weapon before looping more of the length around his neck. With a complex twist of her body she turned, dragging his gun hand to his neck and spinning them back to back. She flipped the guard over her shoulder to land face down on the gravel before he even had a chance to react, then kicked him in the head to make sure he stayed there.

Jerome came striding around from the front of the house. He'd obviously meant to intercept her. The confrontation with the guard had stalled her for just a moment, now he'd cut off her primary route of escape.

Turning on her heel Bethane made for the lawn. Confusion was starting to spread through the party, guests and the guards were clearly agitated. They must have discovered Kartal already, which was no surprise; Jerome had been less than subtle.

She was about to make her way down the lawn to the cliff exfil, use the milling party guests as cover, when a cultured voice rang out behind her.

"Stop that woman, she killed Ekrem!"

A half dozen guards turned toward Jerome's command, eyes following his pointing finger toward Bethane.

"God dammit," she hissed and made for the house at a run.

Dashing through the wide open back doors of the villa, she just had time to notice their embedded agent, his neck twisted unnaturally, on the floor, before two guards appeared at the front entrance, guns at the ready. Thinking on the fly, she swung toward the servants' door, shouldering through it and sending a server and their tray crashing back down the steps toward the kitchen.

Rushing down the stairs and leaping over the stricken waiter, she swept through the bustling kitchen as cries of surprise and outrage erupted around her.

She was making for the underground passage to the garage. The kitchen deliveries came in that way, it had all been in the briefing material and Bethane was truly glad of that. Two security guards appeared at the end of the row Bethane was muscling down, barging cooks and kitchen hands out of her way. The guards' guns were pointed at the ceiling so as not to accidentally shoot the staff while they struggled through the white-coated press toward her. Without breaking stride, Bethane caught up a skillet and, dragging a panicking cook out of the way, bludgeoned the first guard insensible and took the gun out of the second man's hands with the backswing. Grabbing the startled guard's tie she brought her knee up into his stomach and, as he folded, she dragged his head into the steel countertop with a ringing 'bang!' and let him fall insensate to the floor.

Hearing angry voices behind her she turned, barely looking as she threw the skillet overarm toward her pursuers and dragged a bubbling pan of oil onto the floor.

The oil caught on the gas ring and flames leapt in the aisle, sending the kitchen staff into a blind rush away from the blaze and back into the house.

Taking the opportunity, Bethane dashed through the door that would lead her to the underpass into the garage, her shoes ringing hollowly on the concrete as she sprinted the length of the underground corridor.

Careening through the double doors at full tilt she just noticed that a number of the close by lights were out before she registered a slight tug as her purse was dragged neatly out of her hand. It took her a number of strides to arrest her forward charge and spin to face the thief.

"I'll take that, thank you." Jerome sneered from the shadows around the doorway.

Bethane had only a moment to decide; confront a genetically augmented super soldier in hand-to-hand combat while other security personnel bore down on them, or run.

The decision wasn't a hard one, but it left a sour taste in her mouth as she turned and fled deeper into the lower level of the garage.

Finding her car was easy and, since the valets had left the key fob inside, it was unlocked, and the gull-wing door opened smoothly as she slung herself into the driver's seat.

"Control, I've lost the package!" she barked, pressing the ignition button and throwing the car into gear.

"Any chance you can reacquire?" Control asked anxiously.

"Not a chance, that bastard Jerome has it!" Bethane snapped back, reversing the car out and dragging the wheel around as she stomped on the accelerator.

"Tell back-up unit one to stand by, I'm going to need cover."

"Acknowledged."

Flinging the nimble sports car around the curved ramp, Bethane piled through a group of security who, if they'd planted their feet, might have stayed a less disciplined driver. As it was, there was no question of Bethane stopping and the guards dove out of her path rather than be mown down, their guns barking in the night as she raced toward the front gate. The 'crack!' of splintering glass from the tiny rear screen signalled a lucky shot and she twitched the wheel on pure instinct before correcting the slewing car's course and bouncing out of the gate.

Behind her, the cover team staged a rather well-timed and convenient traffic collision. A box truck and high-sided van leaped out of the darkness and hit each other just hard enough to incapacitate the vehicles, hindering any chance of pursuit and obstructing the view of the gate cameras, but not so hard as to cause significant injury to the drivers.

"Well done, Control. Scrub the security system of all traces. Don't take any chances, wipe it all and get out. I'm heading home," she sighed as she sped toward the bridge, the city beyond and the safe house that was her team's rendezvous.

A week later, back in the Papal City, Bethane sat outside Deacon Aurelia's office. Her team had expedited their return, submitted their reports and sat through a lengthy debrief, going over the details of their 'failure' again and again and then, nothing. The intelligence wing of the Vatican had held them at arm's length for days and Bethane had even started wondering what sanctions were being arrayed against them when the call had come to attend the Deacon.

The secretary brought her through and opened the door to the inner office, alerting Aurelia to Bethane's arrival.

"Come in Agent Sciarra," the church superior called brusquely past the young vicar.

Entering the inner office Bethane stood stiffly, not sure what to expect.

"Monsignor," she greeted Aurelia curtly.

The details of the Deacon's acknowledgment by the Pope were classified. It wasn't often a Deacon was awarded the honorific but Aurelia had been an agent of the Church herself and the title, along with her current assignment, had been her reward for some act of service years ago.

"Sit down Agent Sciarra," Aurelia waved vaguely toward a chair. "The details of your report raise a number of questions and I'll be damned if I have the answers."

The Deacon fixed Bethane with a hard eyed glare.

"My report is complete in all aspects," Bethane ventured, hedging her bets until she could be sure where the interview was going.

"Indeed?" the Deacon grunted. "Your report indicates that, not only is a Knight of Camelot guilty of murdering a non-hostile nation's intelligence operative, but also that he was engaged in a covert operation of his own to secure the same data you were tasked with obtaining. So, whilst we have your report on the matter, your control agents' scrub of the site security was so thorough we can't validate it."

"That is correct Monsignor," Bethane nodded simply.

"The story coming out of Camelot is quite different," Aurelia stated dangerously, leaning her elbows on the desk and steepling her fingers.

"They say that, officially, whilst Duke Jerome was present it was simply a matter of personal investment that he was pursuing. That he took no part in the 'incident' save to try and capture the assailant and that they had no knowledge that Ekrem Kartal was anything other than an architect and property developer."

Bethane sat silently as the Deacon's hard grey eyes bored into her.

"Even unofficially, and I've pulled in many favours these past few days to gain this insight, they don't have any real idea either. They knew about the intelligence of course, but they had yet to identify the recipient so, how did Jerome know?"

Bethane breathed an inward sigh of relief. The Deacon had been testing her, looking for cracks in her story. Luckily Bethane had nothing to hide.

"I don't know what's going on, Monsignor," Bethane admitted honestly. "If I had I'd be following it up right now but all I have is—"

"—Jerome," Aurelia finished thoughtfully. "And even a casual surveillance of a senior Knight of the Round Table is a very risky prospect."

"Exactly," Bethane replied sullenly.

Taking a deep breath, Deacon Aurelia sat back in her chair, the old leather creaking gently.

"We'll have to sit on this for now, Agent Sciarra but, rest assured, we have a new task for you and you might be able to keep tabs on Jerome at the same time."

"What's the Op?" Bethane asked eagerly, relieved to be out from under the microscope of Aurelia's scrutiny.

Aurelia drew a thin folder from her desk drawer and tossed it in front of Bethane.

"There's a Squire, Rosalyn Taunton-Savant of Essex. We want you to get eyes on her, gauge her character and the like. All the 'whys' and 'wherefores' are in the briefing packet. The King's Tournament is in a few days and you have until then to be prepped and ready."

"Thank you, Monsignor." Bethane stood, taking the folder and bowing as she backed toward the door. Turing to leave, the Deacon's voice called her to a halt.

"And, Agent Sciarra?"

She turned back to her senior. "Yes Deacon?"

"Two dozen 'Hail Mary's' and thirty 'Our Lord's' as penance for your blasphemy on operation."

The older Deacon's eyes tightened in a sly smile. "Remember, He watches us always."

"Yes Monsignor," Bethane replied curtly. Control was going to pay for not omitting that little detail...

The Wizard

The Wizard walks the world.

Stepping from the battlefield, the wizard slipped easily through the aether. The war behind him was not his to influence, and he slipped from the story like a shadow. No, the inheritors of Camelot must face Morgana, win or lose through their own choices.

Merlin, once Wizard of the Round Table, pursued a greater purpose. The light of stars and possible futures surrounded him as he travelled, his rough battledress shifting, sliding, changing. Even as the wizard exerted his power over his clothes, he trailed his fingers in the ripples of probability, searching for the strands that would lead to the most satisfactory outcomes, the notes that heralded the symphony of balance.

Emerging from the mist, a scent of raw fish assailed his nostrils, shouts and raised voices marking the flow of commerce as people jostled and bartered over the stock at the Tomari Iyumachi fish market.

No-one noticed the tall, white-haired *gaijin* in the crisp grey suit who stepped out of a cloud of steam. Merlin smiled to himself.

I've still got it.

Moving from the building onto the open air portion of the market, the smell of salt and sea carried on the stiff breeze as he slipped past stalls and handcarts laden with the sea's bounty, and out toward the commercial seafront, passing hawkers showing the pride of their wares to passing customers. It took only a matter of minutes for the sage to reach his destination, not any place he had prior knowledge of, but a commercial property that radiated a familiar aura, one he knew of old.

With a thought and a whisper, he transmuted a briefcase into one hand, a black umbrella in the other, and strode confidently to the door. A smart rap on the frame with the umbrella handle and the door opened, a face dressed in consternation peering out.

"*Kon'nichiwa dō saremashita ka.*"

Merlin smiled, "Jonathan Dodd, Tintagel Holdings. I'm here to see someone."

"*Mochiron-chū ni haitte kudasai.*"

"*Dōmo arigatō*" Merlin replied politely, stepping inside.

After only a brief wait in the rather down-at-heel reception area, a young man in a crisp suit entered.

"Mr Dodd?" he enquired in flawless English.

Merlin inclined his head, "At your service."

"Inoue Akihito, I am pleased to meet you. Now, what business brings you here?"

The wizard smiled.

"I require a meeting with *Eien no Hinode*."

The young man stilled, but his smile never wavered.

"I don't know to whom you refer."

Merlin's smile deepened.

"You may inform her that *Ishi no rōjin* is here."

The young man's smile disappeared.

"You cannot..."

Merlin raised his hand, allowing lightning to crawl across the backs of his fingers, and crackle from the corners of his eyes.

"Yes, I can," he replied quietly.

Besides Merlin and the young man and the woman on the front desk, three other people stood in the reception area. Allowing his magic to subside, Merlin noted that none had fled, but all had produced weapons from somewhere, all settling into combat stances, and all of them watching him intently.

"You may tell her it is a 'social visit', merely a formality," he added, reassuringly.

Akihito held his gaze for a moment, twin sai daggers in reverse grip along his forearms held ready. After a tense moment he nodded, straightened, and, in the blink of an eye, secreted the weapons back to wherever they had sprung from.

"Follow me please," he instructed.

Through a busy office space and out toward the rear loading dock, steps quick and purposeful, Akihito hustled Merlin to a freight elevator. With a wave of his hand, Akihito revealed a hidden panel with a dozen extra buttons indicating basement and sub-basement levels. He pressed the button for the lowest level and stepped out of the lift.

As the door closed and the lift rattled into motion, Merlin shook his head at the needless secrecy and theatricality of it all, the veils of normality, the secret security. He chuckled, assuming at least two of these sublevels were for training warriors, the bodyguards of *Eien no Hinode,* the Eternal Sunrise, as some kind of pseudo-religious cult, dedicated to some contrived system of morality and order.

He shrugged, smiling to himself. Not unlike Camelot in that respect...

The lift rattled to a halt, doors opening into an opulent, well-lit reception chamber. Potted bamboo plants, richly upholstered seats, colourful tapestries and a polished wooden floor decorated a room staffed by another, almost identical young woman. She stood at a desk, with two towering guards to either side of the only other door, both wearing full combat gear, topped off with grotesque Oni masks and vicious looking *Naginata*.

Stepping from the lift, Merlin presented himself at the desk. The guards never moved from their posts as the young woman took his briefcase, the smart-phone he had manifested as part of his outfit, and even his patent leather loafers. He was ushered through the sliding paper doors. As he passed between the guards, Merlin could feel the currents of energy flowing through their bodies.

Inside, the Tatami mats underfoot felt warm, as if they had soaked up the radiance of the sun and, for all the world, Merlin could have believed he had just stepped out into the courtyard of a traditional Japanese *minka* or villa. The air was warm and full of the smell of cherry blossom, the tree itself rising from the washed white pebbles in the centre of the yard, leaves stirred by a light breeze.

Water trickled and gurgled from an ornamental fountain. Warm wood and paper panels, decorated with intricate scenes in exquisitely balanced colours, all added to the illusion that he was outside, rather than several storeys underground, not a stone's throw from the docks and fish markets.

"You have some nerve, coming here after what you did," rang an authoritative voice.

"I do," Merlin agreed without pausing. "You might say I am renowned for it. My nerve, that is."

The mats whispered, a sound not unlike a soft broom caressing the wooden floor. Merlin stiffened slightly but forced himself not to betray any sense that he might be ill-at-ease. The inner doors across the yard drew aside, revealing the mistress of the house.

"If it helps at all, I did come to see you first, M'lady *Ugajin*."

Half woman, half snake, *Eien no Hinode* wove forward from the shadowed interior of the minka, her human torso perched atop thirty feet of muscular serpentine body. The vibrant, embroidered silk of her kimono lay draped immodestly across her shoulders, accenting her scales wonderfully. No wide *Obi* cinched her waist, the robe draped open showing an unbroken line of flesh from the Ugajin's throat down to her navel and pubis, where the soft ivory skin met seamlessly with the pale scales of her lower body.

Her soft black hair hung loose, framing her face, her eyes as sharp as blades, fixed on the wizard.

"That is *what* I am, not *who* I am. Shall I call you 'mister human'? Although, you aren't anymore, and haven't been for some time."

The old wizard shook his head, "You never met the mortal me. I doubt you would have been quite so infatuated with him."

Eien inclined her head, hair draping across one vibrant green eye, caressing the soft line of her jaw.

"Was he so different? Were you not always the wily, cunning trickster your legends speak of?"

The old man smiled sadly.

"He was a trickster to be sure, though one without any noble intent to his riddles and games."

Slipping one coil over another Eien shifted her shoulders, the kimono gaping wider.

"But perhaps more honest to himself. His petty avarice unblemished by any stolen nobility?"

"You do me too much credit. There was a time I saw no further than the next stolen meal, the next swindled cup of wine. I had thought my lot hard. The truth was, I sought only the easy way."

"And now that you choose to walk the hard path, has it gotten any easier, old wizard?"

Merlin lifted his chin, gazing into her emerald eyes.

"It is harder, as only those like you can know. However, the food is better, and I spend less time face-down in a pig pen these days."

Rising upon her muscular snake's tail, Eien gestured, arms wide, the silk slipping further down her arms. Her skin seemed filled with light, and her hair stirred like black waves against that glowing shore.

"The modest trappings of immortality, how much could we have had? If we'd hoarded like your dragons, if we'd turned our talents inward? Where would we be now?"

Merlin's breath caught in his throat, his gaze caught in the rapture of her beauty as her hands gracefully traced the fallen hem of the kimono.

"We'd have needed none of it, if only we'd been together. You are as beautiful as when first I saw you, Eien," he said quietly.

Descending in a crash of scales, Eien roughly grasped the fallen silk, creasing and distressing the delicate material, dragging her robe up her arms and around her body.

"You mean that I am as beautiful as the day you left me, *Myrddyn*!" she replied acerbically.

Merlin grimaced.

"Had the choice been mine I would have lain in your coils a while longer but, as you well know, those in our position have obligations, and I was called upon to fulfil mine."

"And look where that led you," the snake-woman sneered. "Betrayed, imprisoned, locked away from the world while your once-apprentice ran rampant!"

Merlin sniffed.

"It was complicated. Her life was ever a harm built of my actions. I had to try to make things right."

"Tell that to *Baba Yaga,* or any of the others among us whom she destroyed! We had a pact, sworn and binding between us, to which she was never bound, and that was your greatest mistake!"

Merlin's eyes hardened.

"Not all, which is why Arthur and Camelot were so important. It was a gamble and, despite the cost, it will pay out. I never claimed to be infallible."

Eien smiled mirthlessly. "From you, that's like saying *'I never admitted to being arrogant'*, it is just assumed that all know it."

The wizard inclined his head in recognition of the score.

"Be that as it may, the subject of Morgana le Fay is soon to be concluded, the chapter closed and bound, which brings me to the reason for my visit."

The scales along the Ugajin's side rustled impatiently.

"You never did show your face without asking something in return. It is a wonder you place so much value upon your mere presence when so few others do."

The muscles of Merlin's jaw tightened in irritation.

"I am here," he began patiently, "in contrition of my failures, to inform you of Morgana's impending doom, and forewarn you of the upheaval it heralds. That power, that she so coveted, hoarded and guarded, will be released once more into the world. A world which, I'm sure you know, remembers how things once were, and is slow to relent its grip upon such memory."

Eien settled back upon a coil, her eyes amused, dark and dangerous.

"And I thank you for the warning, but what would you ask of me in return?"

The old wizard withheld a sigh.

"You have the ear of the dragons, the spirits of the sky and mountains, or those that remain. They in turn have the ear of others. I would have you call a council, to discuss ways in which we might quell the chaos about to be unleashed."

Watching him with dark, glittering eyes, Eien nodded, hair settling on her shoulders in midnight waves, the silk of her kimono brushing the skin of her shoulders and chest.

"No," she said abruptly.

Merlin started.

"No? Do you have any idea what is about to befall this world?"

"By your hand!" the Ugajin snarled, teeth momentarily flashing as fangs between extended, distorted lips.

The old man growled, "Your kind was meant to protect humanity."

Eien rose upon her muscular body, looming above Merlin.

"Humanity, yes. I have no duty to protect your ego, trickster!"

The two immortals glowered at each other under a gentle fall of cherry blossom, a wind stirred from the overflow of building power stirring the pink petals.

"So, you will not be moved on this?" Merlin muttered.

The Ugajin's eyes flashed.

"Not. By. You."

The fluttering petals sank slowly to the ground.

"Fine. By your leave, my lady?" he gestured genteelly to the exit.

"Oh please, do not let me keep you any longer, or at all!" she hissed.

Merlin bowed, then left, ascending the lift in stormy silence and returning through the reception to the street outside. Under a sky wreathed in darkening clouds he reached out to the threads of futures and possible outcomes, seeing himself rejected again and again by the powers behind the world.

Sucking his teeth in disgust, he shifted his focus, dialling it down from grand, sweeping scopes to the briefest moments, the triggers and switches of chance, the places he could tip and shift the balance; the place where the wizard thrived.

If he couldn't convince the powerful, he would simply have to do what he did best, and meddle.

Opening his eyes he stood tall, fixed his tie and stepped, from the street in the harbour, through the aether, to another city, another street.

A ball bounced past with the hollow sound of rubber on asphalt, and a child of six or seven years, hair bedraggled in the light rain, clothes smudged with dirt, followed in heedless pursuit, eyes alight with joy.

Merlin snagged the wayward urchin at the curb, and jerked to a halt. The child looked up at the grey-haired old man in confusion, as a shiny blue saloon car sped through the spot where she would have been, the driver too intent on their phone to react.

A tragedy averted. A parent's grief wiped away.

Raising a bristling eyebrow at the wide-eyed child, Merlin released her, stepping again.

This time to a dark and debris-strewn alley with harsh electric lights overhead, where harsher voices cut through the gloom. A robbery. Brigands laughed as their prey sank, bloodied and scared, to his knees.

With a thought, Merlin switched his prop briefcase to a cane as he strode up to the scene. A blade flashed silver in the late evening murk and the cane swept down, rapping the knuckles of the assailant, the knife dropping unbloodied to the floor.

Turning in shock, the thug caught a swift stroke to the cheek, Merlin employing the cane as a fencer might a rapier. Their victim forgotten, the muggers turned to the wizard, all bravado and belligerence. In the shadows of the alley, Merlin allowed a hint of red to light his eyes, and a lick of flame and brimstone to escape his grinning mouth.

The thugs blanched and ran.

Offering a hand, he helped the staggered businessman to his feet, sending him unsteadily on his way.

A killing averted, a company's moral compass and ethical equilibrium maintained. A police officer assigned to another case where their attention was more urgently required.

From the east, Merlin stepped to Europe, a touch here, an intervention there, preserving, stabilising, saving. Then to Russia, the Middle East, Africa, the Wizard walked the world tipping the scales in the favour of light until...

Vatasha, Macedonia.

Watching from a rooftop by the last rays of the day, the wizard observed as a man hurried down the street, hood up, head down, casting furtive glances behind him. A certain knock on a certain door, and he entered. Inside, quiet voices talked, angry about the reach of the Round Table, its influence. They wondered, if it could cross the ocean and invade Russia on such slight provocation, what was to stop it coming here? They asked, what can be done? They demanded that someone stand up and, ultimately, they decided it would be them.

They did not ask the quiet man in the corner where he got his information from, or why it differed from the words spoken in the news broadcasts, and they did not ask whether it was true.

Merlin felt the anger coming from the cell. He knew that they were not really angry at Camelot, they were angry at themselves, their circumstances, their lot. Their anger made them easily led and, for the quiet man, they were a tool, a weapon gradually primed and pointed toward London.

They didn't have much in the way of weapons, yet. But there was enough explosive material in the basement where they met already to wipe out this building, and all of them with it.

Merlin raised his hand, fingers coming together. A snap of the fingers was all it would take...

But he stopped, let out a deep sigh, and stepped...

London, Regents Park.

Just another suit sipping tea on a brisk October day.

The cafe in the park was quiet and, despite the rain on this cloudy late-autumn morning, Merlin sat outside under an umbrella.

A woman approached, a lady in a pale silver-blue suit, long snowy white hair secured high upon her head. If anyone were to take note of her approach they might find it strange that she wore no shoes. They might find it stranger that, even were it not raining, her bare feet would leave wet footprints behind her.

Merlin stirred his tea without drinking it.

The Lady sat.

"What ails you, my love?"

The wizard tapped the spoon lightly against the rim of his cup.

"They will not meet. Through my fumblings I have poisoned the well, now all will stand alone and it will cost us dear."

Smiling sadly, the Lady reached across to take the old man's hand.

"It is not us it will cost, and that is why you mourn."

With a deep sigh, Merlin nodded.

"You are right, the price will be paid by the mortals, as it ever is, and that is all I sought to avoid."

Sitting back, an arm cast leisurely over the rest of her chair, the Lady crossed her legs, kicking her foot in gentle rhythm.

"You had an idea, an ideal, and that is no surprise, given your position. You exist at a point between us and them, powerful and fallible. I ought to have predicted this, held you apart from them myself, but..."

"But I saw what was to come." Merlin picked up the thread.

"How could I leave the world to fall into such ruin? How could I stand back and let it happen?"

Inclining her head, the Lady agreed.

"You could not, and you should take heart. Things are not as they might have been."

Merlin's palm hit the white-painted cast iron table, rattling his cup in its saucer.

"But they should have been better! I could make it better!"

Leaning forward, the Lady clasped her hands, elbows resting on her knees.

"And how would you achieve it? Would you cull the cruel? Punish the wicked? Set yourself as a righteous god to be obeyed, lest they suffer the consequences of your wrath?"

Merlin scowled.

"Or perhaps a more subtle influence, control the minds of the masses until they have no choice, no individuality, art or agency, until they have the sterile perfection of an ant colony?"

Merlin's face twisted in disgust before he cast his eyes down.

"Have you... interfered?" the Lady asked seriously.

Merlin shrugged.

"Almost. A potential terrorist cell in Macedonia. For a moment I thought to kill them, avoid the harm they would bring."

Her silence brought his head up, his eyes meeting hers, the grey of stone at risk of being crushed by the icy blue of fathomless depths.

"Stones in the pond. You may cast ripples only. Their lives are not for you to take."

Her words were a repeat of a warning drilled into Merlin long, long ago.

"Aye, my Lady." He looked down again at his hands.

The Lady sat back once more, then reached across, took Merlin's teacup and sipped gracefully.

Setting the empty cup down, she stood and held out a pale hand.

"Will you walk me to the ornamental lake?" she asked lightly.

With a deep breath, rubbing his hands down his trouser legs, Merlin stood, taking her hand.

"Of course."

After a few steps, he spoke again.

"Did you ever tell them? That the Lady of the Lake is not bound to the cavern under Camelot? That she can walk abroad if she so chooses?"

The Lady of the Lake laughed, a sound high and clean like crystal bells.

"Of course not. It would bring them too much anxiety. Surely they would be intolerable if they knew."

<u>Squire</u>

"Parry! Return! Disengage! Thrust!"

The sound of steel ringing against steel echoed through the great hall, the high ceiling and glass cases full of antique arms and armour returning the sounds of combat, the squeal of boots on wood, the grunts and cries of effort.

On the mezzanine above, Lady Seraphine Feldon watched Rosalyn Pendragon, Earl Adamant of Essex, teach her new squire, Alyona Klementovich, the basics of the sword.

Watching Rosalyn, her form and stance so familiar, the figures sparring on the wide floor were momentarily replaced in Seraphine's mind by memories of herself and Phillip Christian-Dubois, the previous Earl-Adamant and Rosalyn's knight. She smiled faintly to herself. The two of them had sparred in this very hall, and engaged in other physical pursuits, before Seraphine chose her path as a knight over any romantic entanglements. Phillip had married, and then chosen to be Rosalyn's knight, the weight of acting as mentor to the cloned issue of Mordred le Fay snaring his attention to the point that he passed without children of his own.

In the hall below, Ros addressed some slight inconsistency in Alyona's posture then called 'en garde' and they started the dance again.

With the close of the le Fay campaign, Lady Dubois had renounced her peerage, handing the title and estate to Ros proper (though she still lived in the East wing of the manor) along with her husband's seat at the Round Table, for as long as the Dragon-Slayer proved worthy of it. Rosalyn had come a long way in a brief period of time, and through a great deal of hardship but, to Seraphine's mind, she still had some learning to do before she was truly ready for what was already being expected of her.

Watching the practice below, she smirked. Rosalyn might have corrected Alyona's stance, but Ros herself was still dropping her elbow slightly before her swing, a trait she'd learned from Phillip's tutelage. A habit Seraphine would have to knock out of her.

As a full knight, swordsmanship wasn't exactly on Rosalyn's curriculum, but, having risen so fast, and with Phillip dead, the new knight had needed someone. As her mentor, Seraphine was expected to smooth Ros's rough edges, and there were knights far more practised than Ros who regularly petitioned for Seraphine's instruction, such was her mastery of the blade. It might also do Ros good to fight someone with whom she needn't hold back.

The sound of leather soles whispering across the rich carpet reached her enhanced ears, dragging her from the reverie as surely as a fire-alarm. As was her way, Seraphine waited for the newcomer to announce themself, recognising full-well that the reputation that had grown around her could prove intimidating, even to those in her close company.

"M'lady."

"Bobbi," Seraphine greeted Ros' press agent. "What can I do for you?"

Slim, slick, immaculately turned out, the knight knew Bobbi would be all these things; she didn't need to turn around to see it.

Coming to the mezzanine rail, Bobbi spared a glance for the training taking place down below, then turned, leaning casually on their elbows.

"There are a couple of matters I'd like to discuss, pertaining to the Earl, her new position, her new squire and...some other matters."

Seraphine noted the pause and turned a cool gaze on the agent.

"Is that corduroy?" she grimaced, noting the agent's burgundy suit.

Bobbi blinked. "Yes?"

Seraphine shook her head. "My father had an enduring love of corduroy. Never could stand the stuff myself... So, what is it you need to discuss with me rather than Dame Rosalyn?"

"Just to be clear, I have discussed some of it with Ros, or at least, spoken *at* her about it. I'm coming to you, because she's been less than receptive."

"And, as her mentor, you think she'll take it any better from me?"

"Well, yes. Worst case scenario, you're her superior and can order her to think about it." Bobbi grinned from behind a pair of extravagant horn-rimmed glasses.

The two of them must have been quite a picture, Seraphine considered.

Bobbi, average height for an un-augmented human, slender, in their perfectly tailored suit, with complimenting shirt and a cravat/pocket square set in paisley silk. The tortoiseshell and gold glasses framed large, hazel eyes and the agent's sleek up-do brought the eyes up, just as the highly polished brown brogues brought them down.

For Seraphine's part, she was off-duty so to speak. At formal events she was honour-bound to present in an image that flattered Camelot but, in her down time, outside of her armour, she wore clothes for comfort. Even dressed as she was now in old army boots, thick cotton cargo pants and a simple grey vest, her seven-foot plus stature and the visible augmentations jutting from her limbs commanded attention. And, if not them, the force of her personality and the piercing gaze of her sky-blue retinal implants tended to do the job.

She focussed that stare on Bobbi now, not to intimidate, although that was often a side-effect, but to show that the agent had her full attention as the ringing of steel continued below them.

"So, what did you want to discuss?"

Bobbi produced a Smartphone and stylus, tools of the trade surely, but merely props given the circumstances, something to boost their confidence.

"Well firstly, I'd like to bolster Rosalyn's public image. She was in the public eye all the time during parts of the campaign but, since the ceasefire? She's almost a recluse and, given that she's a decorated war hero, I feel we ought to be making more of that."

Gripping the rail, Seraphine stared out across the hall.

"War isn't pretty, or heroic, or glorious," Seraphine replied tersely. "Mostly you don't win, you just survive. But this conflict? Wars have been fought for territory, politics or ideology, but this one... We faced the sins of our past, and most of the losses we suffered weren't to blades or bullets, but to something far more insidious."

Seraphine's jaw tightened, "There are reasons Rosalyn doesn't want to be in the spotlight, some of them tied to trauma and survivor guilt. The others run deeper."

Bobbi pushed the glasses up their nose.

"Yes but, by withdrawing completely she simply becomes the subject of speculation and rumour. Theories are already appearing on the conspiracy websites. A few more weeks and the community will have worked themselves into a frenzy. Things start appearing in the low end tabloids and, from there? I'm not asking her to be on camera all the time, maybe a couple of guest spots, an interview, a sponsorship deal with some adverts thrown in, that's all," Bobbi explained, tone measured.

"Looking to earn your percentage?" Seraphine clucked, cynically.

Bobbi quirked an eyebrow. "I work for the House of Essex, I get paid no matter what, but the Round Table is down to less than a third of its strength prior to the war. What happens if some other previously unidentified enemy decides to come from the shadows and attack? We don't just need knights, we need M.A.G.E.s, we need soldiers at arms, we need techs, and for that we need inspirational figures like Ros and, I have to say, like yourself. You've not been making so many appearances yourself lately, m'lady."

Seraphine stiffened. "I've been busy."

Retreating a step, Bobbi bowed their head to look at the pad-screen.

"I don't mean to overstep, I know I'm not cleared for everything that happened in Russia but, from what I have read and a few things I've heard, Ros is a hero. As are you all, but at such a young age? She could be a rallying cry, our very own Joan of Arc!"

Seraphine winced. "Yes, well. The less said about her, the better..."

The agent blinked, eyes wide.

"I'll talk to Ros," Seraphine allowed. "Now, what else?"

Tapping at the screen with the stylus, Bobbi sucked at their teeth.

"Not so much a tangent as a parallel issue. Sir Geoffrey Mayland."

Seraphine schooled her expression. "What about him?"

"Well, there were rumours of possible romantic involvement, then he was listed as MIA but subsequently recovered. Now the only official word is that he was gravely injured and is recovering at the Stafford holdings. But, Stafford doesn't have high degree onsite medical, they outsource. So what's going on?"

Seraphine's lips tightened but Bobbi rallied, refusing to allow the knight to intimidate them into silence.

"I can't defuse the questions if I haven't the faintest idea how big the bang could be," they pressed.

Sighing, the Lady of Consett relented.

"Sir Geoffrey conducted himself with courage and honour. However, he was captured and subjected to brutal treatment by the enemy, including, but not limited to, psychological reconditioning. He is presently undergoing assessment at Camelot to ascertain his fitness for duty."

"So, he was brainwashed, and you want to be sure that he isn't anymore?"

Seraphine frowned. "In the very simplest terms, yes. He may present an ongoing threat, the conditioning did a great deal of damage. But he's being given the best of care in his recuperation, and every opportunity to demonstrate his fitness to return, either to duty, or whatever path he so chooses."

"That's a pretty big bang. But not so much, given how many knights turned when the war broke out," Bobbi mused.

Seraphine's expression hardened. "The Table has always encouraged loyalty, even expected it, but we never, ever forced it or manufactured it."

"What about the children bonded to service? They don't have a choice but to repay their parents' debts."

Seraphine's eyes narrowed. "You know as well as I do that they are treated no differently from those that enlist through choice. That they have access to training and education they might not otherwise have access to and that, most importantly, they then do not inherit the same debts. Once their service is done, they are free. If they show promise, they might even be offered a place as a squire. There is no shame or stigma attached to their status."

Bobbi held silent for a time.

"It must have been hard, for some." The agent looked up briefly from the pad. "To hear the stories, the deeds of the great knights of history and think 'I have to live up to that', in a time when it might seem that there's no opportunity."

"Well, we've had plenty of opportunities these past two years. More than many could stomach and enough to satisfy the rest. Now we must heal, tend to the wounds in our hearts and minds, the wounds in ourselves and our society. Much has changed, both within, and without."

"Which is why I need you to convince Ros to get out there!" Bobbi urged. "The public need heroes, now more than ever, and Ros is just that."

Seraphine bridled, visibly reining herself in from an outburst.

"Ros is just a child!" she snapped. "She has been subject to much pain, more than most. Hardship and death have plagued her and, while she is a knight of the Round Table and a veteran of the war, she was unprepared for the demands we placed upon her! Give her the time to heal, the time to come to terms with all that she has been through. A knight she may be, but she is my charge, under my care."

In the face of Seraphine's storm, Bobbi stood implacable.

"You're right," they nodded, tone mild. "She has been through a lot, but she is a knight of Camelot and, now as much as ever, we need her. The people need her. They must be shown that they are safe, that the Table still stands, and stands for the same values it did before. You tell me Ros wasn't prepared for the demands laid on her shoulders? Well boo-fucking-hoo!"

If Seraphine was at all intimidated by Bobbi's outburst the towering knight didn't show it. For their part the slight agent stood, unrelenting with hands on hips, eyes flashing. The standoff held a moment but Bobbi wasn't done.

"People who get caught up in historic, world-changing events rarely are. You're asking me to show empathy? Understanding? Compassion for Rosalyn? I wish I could, I really do, but in the wake of this war, there's an entire nation out there hurting. They need reassurance, they need to know everything's going to be okay, and if it means putting Ros through the misery of public appearances and scrutiny to give them back their confidence in Camelot, to make them feel safe at night? Not only will I put her in the wringer, I'll turn the fucking handle myself!"

Seraphine growled, a rebuke rising in her throat.

"But!" Bobbi held up a hand to still the impending protest, "Trust me when I say I will never let her be ambushed, set up or hung out to dry, not when it is within my power to prevent it. I honestly want her to be seen as the living standard, the benchmark for those who follow."

The senior knight grimaced.

"It will be all the harder for them, now that we have an honest-to-goodness dragon-slayer in our number."

Bobbi blinked in surprise.

"Sorry, what?"

Seraphine cursed under her breath.

"I forgot, you don't have clearance. That situation is still classified."

Folding their arms across the slim, black datapad, Bobbi raised an eyebrow.

"I'm not going to pretend I didn't just hear that. Spill."

Turning from the rail Seraphine stood to her full height. "You would order me?"

Chin thrust out, matching the knight's glare, Bobbi held firm. "Your slip, your mistake, deal with it!"

With a sigh, Seraphine rolled her eyes, returning to the rail.

"The forces of le Fay built a weapon, a biomechanical construct, a Chimaera if you will, inspired by the dragons of legend."

"They built a dragon?"

"Yes."

Bobbi paused.

"And Ros killed it?"

"Yes."

The agent stood in silent thought for a minute.

"How big was it?"

Seraphine sniffed. "About a hundred feet long."

Bobbi's eyes widened. "And did it breathe fire?"

Seraphine nodded.

"And had Gatling guns attached to its forelegs. We have the head, well, the skull in storage."

"That should definitely be on display somewhere, that's awesome."

Seraphine saw the shine in Bobbi's eye as the agent glanced down to where Ros still schooled her new squire.

"Still, that leads us to the last item on my list. There have been rumours, odd things happening, strange creatures spotted. If Camelot's intelligence service knows anything I'd appreciate at least a little heads up."

"What kind of rumours?"

Bobbi let out a wry chuckle. "Locally? Everything from sightings of Black Shuck to the Beast of Bodmin Moor, even a few people claiming to have seen Herne the Hunter in Sherwood Forest. Abroad, there have supposedly been sightings of trolls in the north of Norway and Sweden, not to mention at least one unsubstantiated report of a transport ship being sunk by a sea-serpent. Nothing that's made it to prime-time news yet but, things are getting strange and if you know, I need to know."

Taking a breath through her nose, Seraphine considered the agent's words.

"We're aware," she admitted at last.

"We've been compiling information. Senior M.A.G.E.s Westbrook and Cussler are putting together plans for possible eventualities."

"So, these things are real?"

Seraphine's frosty gaze pinned Bobbi in place, the matter-of-fact tone of her voice more frightening than the full weight of her rage.

"Certain things came to light during the le Fay campaign so, yes they are real and, if we are right, they are just the tip of a terrifying iceberg."

Bobbi swallowed. "I'll, um, see what I can get prepared. You'll keep me informed?"

Seraphine nodded, graciously.

"And you'll talk to Ros, about some appearances?"

Reluctantly Seraphine nodded.

Down in the hall, Rosalyn gave Alyona a few words of encouragement and sent her off to shower. Making a snap decision, Seraphine headed for the grand staircase, leaving Bobbi to blink at her sudden departure.

If she was to talk to Ros about sparring with the national news services, she might as well tie-in a lesson about that dropped elbow at the same time.

"Rosalyn!" she called as the young knight dabbed at her face with a towel, her head coming up like a gazelle sensing a predator, or a lion hearing a challenging roar.

Both knights were unarmoured and bare armed, Seraphine's outfit near mirrored by Rosalyn, wearing an Essex red boiler suit, the top half unzipped and tied at the waist, a simple white vest underneath.

Without breaking stride, Seraphine snatched a long sword from a rack. An expert in arms and history, she recognised the piece, a weapon last used by the Tudors to challenge for the throne of Camelot, a failed uprising fuelled by avarice and petty malice. Still, the Tudors bought their personal weaponry from Spain, the best steel available at the time, and the blade in her hand was still a dangerous weapon, as well as a valuable relic of Camelot's past.

But, steel left too long dulled, its edge worn away by nothing more than time, and a dead blade was a sad thing indeed.

"You can better train your squire by learning your own faults," she declared, swinging the shining steel upward, one hand on the hilt, the other on the pommel, pushing the sword through a punishing arc.

Ros didn't even blink.

Her own sword, loose in her hand was suddenly there, reversed along her forearm, braced to catch Seraphine's at the cross-guard. Stepping forward, Ros shoved the senior knight away, a grin creeping across her lips.

Seraphine was regarded as the finest practitioner of the blade in Camelot. These impromptu sparring sessions were a welcome distraction from the rigours of the political side of life as a knight of the realm.

"Trying to catch me off guard?" Ros questioned her mentor.

Seraphine circled, chuckling.

"Had I meant that, I would not have announced my approach."

Two swords came to guard. Seraphine had drilled Rosalyn about patience, seeking out the perfect moment to strike, and so they circled.

"Bobbi tells me you've been avoiding your public appearances?"

Rosalyn grimaced, but her eyes remained fixed on her opponent.

"I did my part. We won, didn't we?"

Seraphine lunged, a volley of strikes, each met and diverted by Rosalyn's blade.

The senior knight nodded. "Good, you control your emotions well. The fighting may be over, but the fear it has left behind? The people need heroes, Ros."

"Then you do it," Ros replied evenly.

Changing direction, Rosalyn took a turn, thrusting forward, sweeping around and using the clash of blades to spin around again. Her sword described an arc that might have taken Seraphine off at the knee had her mentor not leapt back with a high summersault.

Ros recovered her stance.

"Showy," she commented dryly.

Seraphine gave a slight bow, safe at the distance from any attack Rosalyn might launch.

"I recognise my faults," she said modestly.

"My public persona is well known, I'm the 'Stainless Steel Bitch', incorruptible, humourless, hard and sharp. I go where Camelot seeks to redress insults; I'm not the hero type."

"And I am?" Rosalyn countered as they approached and clashed, a flurry of blows, close and quick.

Looping an arm though Seraphine's guard, Ros turned them back to back, leaning into a throw. Seraphine kicked her legs high, landing on her feet as they came together again, gleaming blades locked, muscles tense, each trying now to out muscle, rather than out manoeuvre, the other.

"You proved it to the Table, now let the public see it." Seraphine spoke through clenched teeth as the two braced and pushed, seeking advantage in the bind.

Slipping a hand from her own sword, Seraphine grabbed Rosalyn's pommel, using the leverage to twist her weapon around.

Sensing the shift, Rosalyn spun away, sword casting a glittering arc as it passed over her head, sweeping over her shoulders and deflecting a blow from Seraphine that might have severed her spine if left unchecked.

They stood, eyes locked, breathing in quick, shallow breaths.

"Is that wise? Given the circumstances of my birth?" Rosalyn asked as the two knights circled once more.

Seraphine allowed herself a frustrated gasp.

"Must it always come to this same argument, Rosalyn?" she danced forward, blade describing silvered arcs in the air before her.

Rosalyn held her ground, a mistake as, at the last instant, Seraphine drew Ros' eyes with a close swing, turning with the blade to sweep the younger knight's legs from under her.

To Rosalyn's credit, she rolled back, kicking away and coming back to her feet with fluid grace.

"The facts don't change, Seraphine," Ros rebuffed. "I am what I am, a genetic experiment based on samples of Mordred le Fay's blood."

Seraphine's face did not betray the smile she felt inside, as she saw, with glacial inevitability, what was about to play out.

Rosalyn's elbow dropped, even as she finished speaking, the first sign of her incoming attack. The student lunged, the mentor catching the approaching blade on her own, the steel shimmering like a serpent, snaking around as Seraphine stepped in. Twisting her body and, with barely an effort, she returned to guard, one sword in each hand, the blades crossing and dropping onto Rosalyn's shoulders, forcing the knight to her knees in submission.

"It always comes back to that, doesn't it? It's your go-to defence," Seraphine shook her head.

"And yet, you have the entire table at your back. Forget, for a moment, that your creation is ranked among the highest of state secrets. If any tabloid or gossipmonger, or enemy of the throne came for you, there's not one knight who would stand by to watch you suffer. Your actions have spoken, your future lies before you. Stop dwelling on a past that was entirely beyond your control."

Recovering the swords, Seraphine took both loosely under one arm and held out her hand to Rosalyn.

Taking her mentor's hand, Ros allowed herself to be drawn to her feet.

The elder knight smirked, "And stop dropping your elbow before you attack, it was a bad habit of Phillip's I never had the chance to correct, don't make me beat it out of you."

Rosalyn let out a chuckle but her expression sobered almost immediately.

Sensing her malaise, Seraphine went on.

"You've risen farther and faster than any knight in history. The public deserves to know why."

"I thought the existence of the dragon was a state secret too," Rosalyn countered.

Seraphine shook her head.

"Slaying the dragon didn't earn you your place, what allowed you to slay the dragon did. Courage, conviction and loyalty. Those things, alongside your latent charisma, are to blame for your meteoric rise."

"Charisma?" Ros questioned playfully.

Seraphine raised an eyebrow.

"Despite Bobbi's tutelage, you are still almost completely without guile. It's frustratingly endearing."

Taking a deep breath, Rosalyn blew it out in a reluctant sigh.

"Alright," she allowed at last, "I'll do it, but I won't be cast as some glittering media darling."

Seraphine let out a snorting laugh.

"I wouldn't worry about that, the public appetite for glitz has waned in favour of competence. They want to know that we can protect them, so I think they'll appreciate a Kevlar-over-Cashmere approach."

Loud applause echoed overhead from the mezzanine.

"Bravo! Bravo!" Bobbi crowed happily, datapad secured under one arm as they clapped.

Ros sighed inwardly. "You recorded that, didn't you?"

"Only the action, your conversation was drowned out by the ringing of steel," the agent replied.

"Why?"

"Are you kidding me?" Bobbi asked in wide-eyed incredulity. "That was gold! Two full knights of the table sparring? It was like a scene from an action movie or something. Just think of the publicity once it *finds* its way onto the info-net!"

The little agent rubbed their chin thoughtfully. "It's only a shame someone's going to say that those were just training blades, real ones would definitely have upped the stakes."

The two knights exchanged glances.

Ros took the Tudor sword carefully from under Seraphine's arms.

"Training blades? You might want to record this Bobbi."

Like a magic trick, the pad was in the agent's hands once more.

The mezzanine was lined and supported by thick, square oak pillars, the hall itself built during the period of the Tudor uprising. The old oak seasoned and aged until it was nearly as hard as iron.

With a sly grin Ros, swung the blade. With a hefty 'thunch!' it bit deeply into the ancient wood, embedding itself firmly, sending black splinters flying.

Bobbi paled, but held the tablet steady as Ros winked slyly at the camera.

Walking past the stunned agent, she turned to Seraphine.

"We really ought to stop using live blades, one of us is going to get hurt one day."

Seraphine smiled. "And on that day, I'll have nothing more to teach you, *squire*."

They laughed as they walked, neither noticing as Bobbi laid a tentative hand on the sword hilt, tugging first gently, then harder and harder, their efforts to remove the sword ultimately futile.

Patrol

"Mission log; after crossing the border at Topol'noe I've followed reports of the targets from Semey to Oskemen and New Bukhtarma. From there they followed the Irtysh River all the way to Lake Zaysan. I feared they would aim to cross the Chinese border at Karaungir but, fortunately, the security there seems to have deterred them. I lost track for three days but headed south-east on a hunch and picked up some stories of large figures stealing livestock in the night around Oichilik."

He stopped for a moment and sighed before continuing.

"I suspect they've crossed the mountains at Khrebet and will follow the border toward Zhalanashkol. If I'm right I can cut through Alakol and catch up to them somewhere south of Dzerzhinskoye."

Royston Glasbury, Baron of Tonbridge, Knight of the Round Table, mentally deactivated the recorder. After the final battle of the Le Fay campaign, cleanup had been a high priority for the knights of Camelot, tracking down the fleeing agents, soldiers, sorcerers and monsters of Morgana le Fay's forces. Capture, contain or, if no other option proved viable, kill, was the order.

Many had fled south toward the Caucasus region. When Royston received orders to track a large group headed east, he'd expected them to veer north to less densely populated country, not south into the steppes and plains of the Middle East and northern Asia.

The states that had managed to separate from Morgana's Russia existed trapped between the looming shadow of imminent invasion from the north and the sceptical suspicions that they'd already allied themselves that way from the south. Stuck in the middle, they had fared little better than their northern neighbours.

International diplomacy wasn't Royston's bag. A skilled marksman, he preferred looking at his problems through the simple point-and-click solution of his scope than trying to play the game of politics. The war had been a time of fear, horror and doubt but, after the initial betrayal, it had been a time of simple solutions for Royston. It had also been a crucible that fired the insecure young boy that he had been into the skilled and assured knight who now surveyed the flat plains of Kazakhstan.

Tempered as he was, he'd lost that part of him that doubted his place as a squire, and then a knight, but not his easy nature and infectious humour. Which was why this current assignment was so hard on him. He might be fully six feet eight inches of genetically and bionically enhanced super-soldier, but that couldn't stop the pangs of loneliness that this sometimes desolate landscape engendered. The Table had lost much to the war, now its resources were stretched thin in both hunting Morgana's monsters and rebuilding the ruined states she'd left behind. Still, Royston missed his friends.

But, he was the arrow, and his target lay ahead. It was up to him to ensure his flight was swift and his aim was true.

"Vehicle on approach," Royston's C.T.E.E.D., re-designated 'Artemis', reported.

The young knight shook himself from his reverie, asking absently, "Anyone we know?"

"Commander Altynai Ospanova, Kazakhstan State Security Service. Maybe she's actually going to arrest us this time," the C.T.E.E.D. replied dourly.

Royston loved his mount. The cybernetic horse was one of the most coveted trappings of a knight of the Round Table but... Tonbridge was a poor seat, and he'd inherited the estate's second generation, a service line famed for their tendency toward paranoia and pessimism.

"She's not going to arrest us, we have her government's permission to be here," the knight replied for the umpteenth time.

"They can always change their mind. The longer this chase takes, the more the probability percentage increases."

A chunky four-wheel drive car, not unlike an old pattern Land Rover, chugged to a halt a few metres away. The driver, a broad-shouldered, athletic woman with square, handsome features, stepped out. Her trench coat fluttered in a short-lived breeze that stirred the pale gold grasses of the plain, briefly revealing the heavy pistol strapped to her hip. Kazakhstan didn't have the higher levels of technology, genetics and bionics enjoyed by Camelot and other nations so, in response to the unknowable threats from the north, they'd invested in heavy, though basic, firepower for their special services.

Not slowing her brisk pace, she pulled a packet of the local cigarettes from her pocket, sliding one out to slip between her lips and lighting it with practised movements. Royston could smell the oily smoke from the rough tobacco even as she approached. Sliding out of his saddle, he dropped lightly to the ground, armour absorbing the impact and deadening any sound he might have otherwise made. Raising his hands, he removed his helmet, better to meet his local liaison face-to-face.

"How do you track me so efficiently?" he asked breezily in perfect Kazakh, the language uploaded to his neural implants for just this reason.

The Commander frowned.

"Simple, I slipped a tracking device up your horse's arse."

Artemis stiffened, but Royston just smiled. Even his ageing C.T.E.E.D. could detect any tracking system the Kazakhstani techs could produce.

Taking a long drag and blowing smoke impatiently, Altynai glared at the horizon.

"No, our people don't know much about the wider world. My department has simply instructed all police precincts in this area to forward any reports of a giant black man on a robot horse to me. Given the nature of the locals, I'm surprised you haven't been shot at more."

Royston grinned. "I keep my distance, no need to cause an incident."

The Kazakh Special Services officer eyed him warily, trying to decide if he was being serious before replying.

"You may, but these creatures you're following? They do not. I have eighteen corpses in morgues along their trail, the same again in missing persons, and thirty in a hospital back in Oktyabrskij."

Royston nodded soberly. "And that's what confuses me. You told me that those people confronted the targets, an armed mob and yet, they were incapacitated, not killed. That doesn't match up with what I know of Morgana's shock-troops."

"Yes, these O.R.C.'s you spoke of."

Royston's friend, Nicholaeos Westbrook, had designated the misshapen bionically-enhanced shock troops as *Organic Re-sequenced Commandos* back at the start of the war. 'O.R.C.s' for short, and the name had stuck.

He stifled a grin, remembering how Rosalyn had accused Nicholaeos of playing fantasy roleplay games as a kid.

"How can six of these things take out thirty armed farmers? I wouldn't lay odds that our best soldiers could do such a thing, not without killing somebody at least," Altynai ventured thoughtfully.

"I've seen your farmers. I don't think *I* could do it," Royston quipped.

"Still, those people ought to be dead, not recovering in hospital. It makes no sense, why them and not the others?"

"We find them and you can ask them. Oh, this arrived for you, by carrier crow of all things."

The agent held out a small data-chip."

"He's a raven," Royston replied distractedly, taking the chip and slipping it into a slot in his helmet.

"I'll review it on the ride, if we move we might be able to get ahead of them."

Stepping into the stirrup, he swung up into the saddle. "Try to keep up."

"Hey!" Ospanova stopped him. "I'm glad of your help, Sir Knight, but don't go thinking I'm some damsel in distress. I can take care of myself."

The open landscape stretched out around Royston as he rode. With a thought, he initiated the playback on the data-chip.

"Royston," the voice of Cassie Cussler, Court Magician, sounded through his helmet comms.

"I hope this reaches to you in time, I'm sending it via Eric to be sure."

The raven who had delivered the chip was her beloved cyber-familiar, who she had rebuilt after Morgana was defeated.

Royston grinned. Each knight had a locator beacon, but Kazakhstan didn't exactly have the information and communication infrastructure for them to be effective. Hell, neither did Russia under Morgana's rule, but Camelot was taking steps to fix that.

"We've observed some anomalies in the behaviour of the O.R.C's in our custody. It seems that, as well as twisting their bodies, they were subject to extensive psychological conditioning to assure their loyalty and insulate them from the brutality Morgana expected of them."

The pale sun was headed for the horizon in the West, darkness creeping toward the sky in the East.

"Initially they exhibit periods of extreme emotional instability, rage, grief etcetera, but!" Cassie sounded excited, "Some of them have come out the other side with reason, logic and— get this— remorse and empathy for what they've done! We might never be able to reverse the procedures enacted on their bodies, but we might be able to save their minds."

Royston scowled.

'Tell that to the eighteen dead civilians behind me,' he thought, but, even then, he couldn't discount the events in Oktyabrskij. Thirty spared, for seemingly no reason.

He'd never considered himself given over to philosophy, but it seemed to the young knight that, from the moment he'd left on this mission, the outcome would be violence, as red with blood as the Western sky. Now Cassie offered him another option, but unsure, unknown, an outcome swathed in uncertainty, well represented by the darkening East. And him, sat squarely in the middle, at the whim of fate and chance.

For a moment he was that boy again, his efforts to please his elders a desperate attempt to cover his own lack of confidence. He wished John were here, or Geoff, Ros, heck, even Belvarre! Someone to take the decision out of his hands. Altynai had called him a 'man' which, given his stature and scars, was not an unreasonable assumption, but he'd barely begun his tenure as a squire when the war began. Maybe, for all the improvements 'sand surgery, for all the armour, the status and violence he'd accrued and been subjected to since, that boy was still inside him, still scared of screwing things up and receiving his liege's ire...

Cassie's message played on, as his mind wandered through his doubts, talking about possible degradation of the logic and impulse control centres of the subjects' brains, but he came back to himself for her summation.

"I'm not saying this will end peacefully, and I wouldn't want you to walk into an ambush expecting a hug and a sharing circle," he could hear the worry behind her flippant words, "but maybe don't shoot them on sight, okay?"

He took a deep breath through his nose, smelling the plastic sterility of his helmet's scrubbers.

"Okay," he said softly in reply, though she couldn't possibly hear him, all the way away in Camelot.

His local comm chimed at an incoming signal. With a twitch of his cheek, he opened the channel.

"Sir Knight!" Altynai's tone was clipped, urgent.

"What is it, Commander?" Royston replied easily.

"A report from a station to our east, local children have found something in the woods, sounds like one of your Orcs. We should divert and investigate."

"Copy that, range and bearing?"

The young knight suspected he heard a slight grin in the security officer's voice as she replied, "Oh no you don't. The people there are likely twitchy enough, we can't have you causing an incident if you arrive before me. Now let's see if you can keep up!"

With a rumbling roar, the ageing four-wheel drive pulled past in the other lane, rattling its way into the lead.

"Of course, after you," Royston allowed, graciously.

A half hour later, they had travelled from the plains into an area of farmlands studded with low, scrubby trees. A series of official vehicles topped with red/blue lights led them from a farmyard along rough tracks into the trees. The officers stationed along the route reacted to Altynai's badge with wide-eyed surprise, but to Royston astride his mount with open-mouthed amazement.

In a clearing, they arrived at the scene of the disturbance. Floodlights had been brought in to stave off the oncoming night, and Royston sensed that the officials here processing the scene were more than glad of them.

Dismounting, he swept practised eyes around. The clearing was larger than it might previously have been, short trees had been uprooted, smashed and ripped from the ground, which had been gouged and rent, as if by an excavator piloted by a maniac. His eyes detected signs of small arms fire. Well, if you could regard the automatic cannons that had been orc standard issue as 'small'.

In the middle of the torn up clearing, a white tent had been erected, guards on post by the door. Altynai took a long drag on a new cigarette, flicked the burning end away and slipped the unsmoked length back into the pack, then she gestured for Royston to follow her.

She led the way to the tent, holding the flap as the young knight ducked inside, hunched, lest he disturb the tent and the work going on within. Three people in white coveralls and dust masks, their boots sheathed in blue plastic slippers, moved around the sprawled body of one of Morgana le Fay's chosen shock troopers.

Royston frowned, thoroughly confused.

"Who killed it?" he asked aloud.

"We don't know," Altynai replied. "The first report we have is that some kids heard a disturbance in the woods. When they came to look they found this, ran back to the nearby farmhouse, and brought a parent who called the nearby station. The responding officers called for forensics, mistakenly assuming a human body was involved and from there it bounced to us. The current theory is maybe a falling out or disagreement among the group. You said they were violent, unstable."

Royston settled down into a crouch, sitting on his heels.

"What's the timeframe?" he asked.

"Earlier this afternoon."

Royston rubbed a hand across his chin, "That doesn't track, they've been moving under the cover of darkness."

"We have signs of a camp, about two-hundred yards to the east. Why they came over here, and did this..." the commander shrugged.

"Maybe..." Royston muttered thoughtfully.

The thread of uncertainty that had crawled into his head was, more and more, starting to feel like the Lambton Wyrm, coiled in the darkness at the bottom of its well, growing day by day.

He let his gaze fall on the body. A violent death no doubt, whether by bullet or blade? Probably both, the damage was so extensive.

"And then there were five," he mused thoughtfully. "Would you mind if I walked the perimeter?"

"As long as you report back anything you find," Altynai replied with a shrug.

Outside the tent, Royston heard an unfamiliar voice ask "Who the hell was *that*?" before Altynai's characteristic abruptness replied "He's a consultant, and that's all you need to know."

He smiled to himself, striding into the darkness.

At the edge of the clearing, he let the plate in the side of his head slide open, the mechanical monocle of his targeting systems slipping into place over his lead eye. He could use the night vision systems in his helmet but, as his liaison had suggested, these officers were twitchy enough.

Stepping out of the glare of the spotlights, he moved through the deeper darkness of the dense trees, eyes down, sweeping left to right, making no more sound than a breath of wind.

He concentrated on the southern edge, sweeping east to west, then moving out and backtracking. He found the trail of the O.R.C. s straight away, they'd trampled a swathe of brush before, apparently, remembering themselves and moving with more caution, but he had a hunch he was looking for...

There. A tree marked with what looked like claw marks, the runnels fresh-carved in the wood and spaced wider than his fingers could spread and, further on...

Orcs might be monstrous people, but they were still just people.

They did not have claws.

"Commander Ospanova," he spoke into an open comm channel.

"Sir Glasbury?" she responded.

"You might want to see this, come to my position, and bring light and a plaster kit."

He waited in silence until she arrived, two other officers in tow, torches sweeping the ground.

"There." He pointed without tearing his eyes from the imprint.

An indentation in the ground. Under the light of the torches he could see more clearly, a paw, possibly ursine, probably feline, maybe eighteen inches across, and the depression in the spongy ground indicating a creature massing out at over seven-hundred kilos, maybe fifteen-hundred pounds.

He caught Commander Ospanova's eye.

"I think we have a bigger problem than a couple of O.R.C.'s." he said quietly. "I need to move, quickly." Altynai's raised eyebrow was query enough.

"We should have been ahead of them. If they've picked up their pace, then I need to pick up mine, too."

Straightening the front of her jacket, the commander glanced around at the darkening trees.

"Then what are we waiting for? I'll radio ahead, try to arrange some backup from the military."

Hurrying back to the clearing, Royston vaulted up into Artemis's saddle. With a light touch, he opened a panel located at the base of the C.T.E.E.D.'s neck.

"Here," he held out a small flatscreen device, "I'll follow the trail, you follow on the road, track me with this."

"You sure?" she asked, holding the slim device sceptically.

Royston nodded sharply.

"We need to know what's going on here. If another of Morgana's monsters is on the loose..." he let the statement tail off.

"Well, good luck, don't go too far. And wait for that backup if you have the option," she called the last over her shoulder, hurrying for her car.

Spurring Artemis into a gallop, Royston used his optical implants to locate and follow the trail left by the orc soldiers.

The first few hundred yards was easy, there were tracks and damage to the low-lying trees and foliage from the orcs themselves, and something bigger, heavier. Whether Morgana's shock troops were herding, chasing or fleeing the thing was a question Royston dismissed from his mind. He had no cause to complicate things right now; stay on target, get them in the crosshairs first, then answer the questions.

Breaking from the trees, Artemis' voice sounded in his ear.

"Is this wise?"

"Define 'this'?" Royston replied through gritted teeth.

"Continuing the pursuit alone when an unknown element, possibly an incredibly dangerous one, has been introduced," the C.T.E.E.D. answered dourly.

The young knight grimaced. "Commander Ospanova is coordinating military support, but that does us no good if we can't find the thing. I'm relieved that at least we can rule out another dragon."

"Really?" Artemis sounded less than enthusiastic, "Given Morgana's flare for the dramatic and the sheer variety of exotic monsters in human mythology, I'd postulate it was an even more terrifying prospect."

"You are just a laugh a minute, you know that?" Royston observed dryly.

"Don't blame me, I'm just a machine. It's not my fault how I was programmed."

"Yes well, give me some quiet to think, or I'll have your programming uploaded to a toaster when we get back."

"Well that's just charming," the cyborg muttered glumly.

The tracks led out into the grasslands, nothing but rolling plains and long grass to be seen for miles on either side, but up ahead...

"Where were we just now?" Royston asked.

"Local intelligence has the nearest settlement as Yntaly."

Royston nodded and selected the radio band he and Ospanova used for direct communication.

"Ospanova, you out there?"

"You don't get rid of me that easily. What do you have?" came the crackling reply.

"It looks like the targets took to the hills, literally. There's a river valley south of Yntaly…"

"The Tente," the security officer cut in, "not exactly the easiest route to take, but if you wanted to get out of sight…"

The channel went quiet for a moment.

"The Tente has tributaries running into it. The first is maybe twenty kilometres from where you are, there are more further down but—" her voice was hard, the channel momentarily clearing. "—each one has a town on it and we've had no reports of incidents or sightings and, given how fast your friends move, I'd have expected something. For whatever reason, there's a good chance that they're still in there."

"But why, why have they gone to ground? Unless…" Royston bit back a curse. "Whatever else is out there, whatever they were hunting, is now hunting them."

"Are you sure about that?" Ospanova countered.

Royston replied "It's the only thing that makes sense. Whatever this is, it's responsible for those eighteen bodies. When the orcs caught up with it, engaged it, it killed one of them. Now they've led it into these hills to try and get it away from the towns and finish the job."

Altynai's reply was matter-of-fact.

"So it kills them, you kill it. What's the problem?"

Royston was more than a little taken aback by the surety in her voice.

"Well firstly, if it can kill them as a group, what's to say it can't kill me on my own? And, secondly…" he sighed, "If they have tried to preserve life and kill this creature as a threat to innocents, I'm going to have to try and save them, aren't I?"

It wasn't really a question. The knights' code of honour demanded no less.

Over the radio connection Royston could hear Altynai suck air through her teeth.

"I will never understand you knights," she muttered. "Alright, I will circle around, approach from the south. It will take me most of the night, I might not reach you until dawn."

Royston hesitated. The agent, like any warrior, had her pride, but...

"You shouldn't come in alone," he said finally.

"And you should?" she rebuked him but then, "Don't worry about me, I'm the one bringing the backup, remember?"

The young knight smiled in the darkness.

"Alright. I'll be in touch. See you on the other side."

The hillside of the river valley was dusted with the same low dense trees as the plains. Royston dismounted after an hour, leading Artemis on foot to preserve as much stealth as possible.

Sudden distant gunfire echoed from the valley walls accompanied by a blood-chilling roar.

"Come on, Artemis!" Royston ordered.

His augmented legs carried him swiftly and silently through the forest even as his eyesight guided him. After a few hundred metres he stopped, listening for the sounds of combat.

Silence.

"Shit!" he swore vehemently and scanned his head left and right, his helmet systems shifting through visual spectra as the audio pickups strained to hear anything.

A crack of branches nearby made the young knight crouch low. Artemis stepped up silently beside him.

"What is that?" he murmured into his suit's sub-vox comm.

"Heat signature. Large, mobile. Probability that it's the unidentified target? High." Artemis replied through the suit systems.

The young knight worried his lower lip a moment. His body had been augmented, maybe not as much as his friends in the richer houses, but he was much taller and stronger than any human his age. He was also clad in a tailored suit of armour, which played host to a catalogue of enhanced systems designed for everything from combat to disaster response. His C.T.E.E.D. Artemis acted as his transport, support vehicle and armoury, carrying his long-rifle, bow and arrows and, should he really need them, sword and shield. He had all the tools he should need to hand. What he needed was something none of them could supply; guidance.

He took a deep breath to calm his nerves and try to stem the swell of uncertainty.

What were the options?

If he was to use his rifle, the best position for a shot would be the opposite wall of the valley.

Going toe-to-toe with an unknown creature that outmassed him by more than a hundred-percent again? Probably not the best idea.

Moving quietly to Artemis, he lifted his quiver and compound-bow. The arrows had different heads for a range of effects, and the bow itself was near a two-hundred and fifty pound draw.

"Wait here," he ordered and slipped into the night.

Knights are supposed to charge unheeding into battle, unafraid and valiant, he thought as he stalked slowly forward. It was one of the lessons his liege, Sir Leopold, had drummed into him, all the while having him trained and augmented as a marksman to win his poor country seat recognition in the King's games.

His hypocrisy didn't end there of course. Ultimately Leopold had defected to Morgana's side at the outset of the war, so his lessons about loyalty were suspect too.

Of course, the face of warfare had changed, first with the so-called 'Great' wars of the early 20th century, now again with Morgana, introducing monsters and magic into the mix. Royston held out little hope that *that* particular genie was going back into its bottle any time soon.

Picking his way slowly through the trees, these thoughts turning over in his head, he missed the noises gradually growing louder and louder as they echoed through the woods. The shift of a large body on the forest floor, the huff and growl of breath and the grate and grind of teeth against bone.

A cloud, gently sculling across the sky, cleared the moon momentarily and, in that instant, the pale blue light washed across a scene out of a nightmare.

At first Royston couldn't quite identify the white shapes that glistened and jiggled under the moon's glow, but then it struck him.

Exposed bones and massive teeth.

Half a ravaged orc carcass in its mighty paws, Royston found himself staring, through the thinning branches, at three sets of glowering eyes. A giant lion's head, fangs like sabres, worried at the meat held in the creature's carving-knife claws. Even as it ripped a hunk of flesh away, a second head, a goat's head, rectangular pupils stretching its irises, let out a shrill, shredding bleat and bent forward to the feast. The creak and rustle of leathery wings almost masked a sinister hissing as a massive snake coiled forward. Royston could barely believe it but, when the beast shifted its massive bulk forward to bear down on its prey, the snake was attached, continuing the spine in place of the expected lashing lion's tail.

Pictures of the Chimaera had graced some of the pages of his history books, those dedicated to Greek myth anyway. Those beasts had been depicted as misshapen, yes but, in their way, sleek and powerful. This creature was a horror. As another cloud sculled aside, the moon revealed patches of scabrous fur, the flesh beneath almost rotten. The snake's scales, rather than shining and lustrous, seemed dry and brittle. Its features were lumpy and distorted, as mismatched as its body-parts. Royston was for a moment glad of the air filters in his helmet; the readout indicated trace toxins and necrosis that suggested a truly vile smell.

He'd faced a dragon, from five-hundred metres away, through the sights of his rifle. This creature was nowhere near as big, but it was a hell of a lot closer.

A tremor ran through his shoulders to his hands. He swallowed hard, crushing the rising fear down before it affected his aim, and drew the compound bow. The arrow was flared, with a sharp, crossed cutting head based on a hunting arrow, but behind the head and embedded in the shaft, a lump of depleted uranium gave the arrow the power to punch through body armour and bone. At full draw, the pulleys mounted at the top and bottom of the bow eased the strain. Two-hundred and fifty pounds of draw, reduced to less than four, as he sighted down the shaft.

With a sigh of released breath, he let the shaft fly, the 'thunk' of the string sounding impossibly loud in the night.

The beast reacted instantly, head rising. The head of the arrow, so clear in Royston's enhanced vision, glanced across the patchy, sandy fur of the lion's head, the shaft splintering as it struck, pieces falling to the ground, leaving only a shallow graze.

The Chimaera roared, all three heads sweeping around, seeking the source of the attack.

Impossible, Royston thought, *that arrow could have punched through a tank!*

Switching tack, he selected a high-explosive arrow and drew, only the creaking of the pulleys betraying his position.

At the point of release, a hand snaked out, viper fast, and snatched the arrow from the string. The bow let out a dull 'thud' as it dry-fired. The Chimaera's three heads snapped around, gazing into the night seemingly right into Royston's own.

A huge hand clapped on his shoulder, dragging him around. Now Royston was face-to-face in the dark with another monster, the brutal features of an orc, one of Morgana's savage shock troops. The knight stared at the orc for what seemed like an age before, behind them, the Chimaera let out a bellow, a bleat and a sibilant hiss, three throats calling as one. With a gout of noxious gas, the heads belched out a stream of fire, spitting flame in a bright curtain to shield it from further attack.

The orc frowned, its face furious in the light from the flames, and spoke one word.

"*Begat.*"

Run.

Cowardice is not the way of a knight, Royston knew this lesson. However neither was stupidity.

The advantage of surprise lost, the knight rose on powerful legs, sprinting after the orc who had already run back through the trees.

"Artemis," he called into their shared comm channel, "I'm compromised, activate escape and evasion protocols and rendezvous at first opportunity."

"Acknowledged, I knew this was a bad idea," the C.T.E.E.D. replied sulkily.

In the dark, Royston relied on motion and heat tracking to follow the orc down the ever increasing incline. The crash and roar of the Chimaera sounded from close behind, the thump of its ragged wings lifting it in what the knight assumed were long assisted jumps. That must have been how it avoided detection. Firstly, they hadn't known to look for it; in the towns, it left no tracks on concrete or tarmac, and it leapt away far enough they never picked up the trail.

Momentum carried Royston faster, ducking and dodging through the close packed trees which leapt out of the darkness in the sullen green tones of his night vision.

A loud thump announced the monster landing close behind. He risked a glance over his shoulder to see the beast swipe at his back. With an involuntary cry, he leapt forward, smashing through a tree as thick as his thigh, falling into a forward roll. His armour sounded caution alarms, icons flashing on the HUD. His bow was wrenched from his grasp, left hanging on some outstretched tree limb as he pushed faster, jinking to evade the crashing monster snarling at his back. Then, with a 'Whuff' of downdraft, it was gone.

Still Royston ran, coming to a halt only inches from a low cliff staring down into the turbid waters of the rushing river, white water glowing in the moonlight. Next to him, the orc stood, chest heaving, staring out into the night.

Royston hesitated, uncertain, before speaking.

"Is it gone?" he asked.

The creature took a deep breath.

"No," it replied simply.

As if awaiting the cue, the Chimaera landed, the ground trembling beneath its claws.

Thrusting his arms forward, Royston presented the small-arms in his bracers, ready to fire.

"Wait!" the orc cautioned, reaching for him, but it was too late.

Royston's weapons barked over the sound of rushing water and the rumble of the snarling monster, rounds stitching impacts, sending out tufts of ragged fur, across the creature's faces, targeting the eyes and soft tissues.

The beast recoiled for a split second, then, with a roar of defiance, it hooked a forepaw around a thick tree, a swipe of its powerful claw sending branches, trunk and roots tumbling toward knight and orc both.

Caught off-guard, the tree slammed into them, carrying them tumbling over the cliff to plummet to the rushing water below.

Royston's systems screamed for a moment before his in-helm screen stuttered and died, leaving him in total blackness.

Tossed in the current, battered by rock and water he started to panic, no idea how deep or how far he'd travelled. The water might carry him to the delta, if he didn't suffocate first.

A jolt, and the world stopped spinning. The water still tugged at him, but with no more unexpected impacts, no spiralling sensation. He was caught, snagged on something.

Breathing rapidly, he tried to calm himself. If he moved too fast he might come unstuck, but the sensation of moisture from the air recyclers in his armour was panicking him. Drawing a shuddering breath, he stilled his mind, listening to his body. Which of his long limbs stirred with the current, where was the sense of tension, the anchor point?

Tension in his leg. Curling against the flow of water he grasped his thigh, working his hands higher and higher. The insulation in his armour kept the cold of the water out, but still he shook, unable to ignore the idea of trying this with his lungs screaming for air. His hands trembled from the cold.

He reached his ankle, finding something solid and round, maybe a branch? In that moment, something smashed into his shoulder, flinging him back. In a panic he kicked out, trying to secure his other foot, feeling his tenuous anchor point slipping.

Motion, jostling, falling and a sudden impact.

He sensed he was out of the water. All was still and he could feel hard ground beneath him. Rolling over, he sat up, snatching at his helmet clasps frantically to remove the dead piece.

Gasping for breath, he rocked gently, letting the panic fade, the anxiety drain away.

"That was ill-advised," his 'saviour' coughed around the words in a voice rough with river water.

"It's not every day an animal is immune to a depleted uranium shaft," Royston snapped back.

He raised his head and flinched.

The orc glared at him, yellow irises burning with suppressed anger, squared jaw tense, mismatched tusks peeking from behind its lower lip. It wore a knot of braids, woven tight behind its head, and had a brutal looking scar running from curled top lip beneath its pug nose and on to its pointed ear.

In the dark Royston wasn't sure, but the monster's skin-tone seemed to be a muddy grey, unless it wore the same camo paint across its face, broad shoulders and down its long, muscular arms. Its gear was the universal black combat dress of the le Fay Special Forces, sleeveless tac vest, combat trousers and heavy boots. This O.R.C. had added to this however, with pieces of metal, maybe armour plate, bound to its arms, body and shins with what looked like leather straps from a horse's bridle and harness, in a kind of rudimentary splint mail.

A bandolier crossed its torso, mostly empty, but the shells if did hold were large, befitting the oversized rifle slung across the orc's back. The weapons paired with a crude axe which seemed to be no more than a sheet of torn tank-plating tied with more harness leather to a thick tree-limb.

"You're staring," the creature grunted brusquely.

Royston recovered himself.

"I'm sorry. I've never been this close to one of you without them trying to tear me to pieces."

"Give me a reason and I'll oblige you," the orc answered distractedly, head up, sniffing the air.

"What are you doing?" Royston asked.

The orc glowered at him. "I'm figuring out where we are. I think the river has taken us maybe a mile back toward the delta."

"It's an alluvial fan," Royston muttered, drawing his legs up and hugging his knees.

The orc frowned, the expression first angry, then confused.

"What's wrong, are you hurt?" it demanded.

The young knight shook his head, "No, I'm just..."

The orc sniffed again.

"How old are you?"

Royston looked up, meeting the enquiring stare.

"Old enough," he insisted.

The orc straightened, stepping back.

"You're just a child. What are you, sixteen?"

Royston surged to his feet.

"I am Sir Royston Glasbury, Baron of Tonbridge and Knight of the Round Table!"

The orc gave a rough chuckle, "And that's going to save you now, is it? Half drowned, no real weapons to speak of, facing down one of Morgana's monsters."

"Maybe more than one," Royston growled. "But you're wrong, I'm not 'half drowned', I'm fine. My armour seals held."

The big brute shrugged. "You didn't seem in a hurry to drag yourself from the bottom of the river."

Royston snatched up his helmet. "My display malfunctioned, I was disoriented, okay? It's nothing a few minutes with Artemis won't fix."

"Uh huh," the orc nodded, "and where is this Artemis?"

"I..." Royston began.

The truth was, without the visor display he didn't know, and the damage to the helmet had killed his comms too.

"*Fuck!*" he yelled into the night, starting to pace.

The orc was right. His armour was broken, he had no access to its more advanced tracking functions, his weapons were lost, or with his horse, which he didn't have either.

"What are you even doing here *malen'kiy*?"

Little one, his translation software provided.

"I'm here for you and your unit," he replied, his voice tight and terse.

"Uh-huh, on what orders?"

The young knight's eyes narrowed. If the orc were going to come at him, it would be now.

"Contain, capture... or kill."

The orc huffed an amused breath through its nose.

"Then the chimaera has done you a favour. It has killed two of mine so far, and we have yet to effectively wound it, no matter what we try. I am *Stárshiy Serzhánt Darya Basov.*"

The creature was matter-of-fact, almost amused in a fatalistic kind of way, its voice hard-edged but accent lilting. It didn't seem about to attack him.

"You ambushed it, outside the farm," Royston ventured.

Darya nodded. "First time we caught up to it since the border with China. We hit it with everything we had, for all the good it did us. Now you see why I didn't want you to use your little pop-guns, you only pissed it off."

Royston couldn't suppress a smirk.

"What's so funny?" the orc demanded.

"Nothing," Royston shook his head. "I just never thought of your kind having names beyond 'Urg' of 'Gruk', that's all."

A wide pink tongue licked a long yellow tusk.

"I wasn't born like this, and I wasn't grown in a tube like that monster out there. I was a real soldier once, before they did this to me."

"What's it like?" Royston asked before he could stop himself.

Darya's eyes fixed on him and, for the first time, they seemed on the verge of violence. Then, taking a deep breath, the orc spoke.

"Between the re-education programme, the surgery, the drugs and whatever else, I don't remember much. What I do remember is like a nightmare."

"So why volunteer?"

Again, Royston's mouth seemed to be on automatic, bypassing his sense of tact.

Darya let out a deep, dark guffaw.

"Volunteer? Didn't you know, little knight? We were all 'volunteers' in Morgana's army, all of us, volunteered for everything, whether we wanted it or not."

Royston blinked, struggling for the right words.

"I'm sorry."

The orc shrugged. "It's not all bad, no more unwelcome advances from arrogant men."

Royston blinked. He'd completely missed it in the dark and with the bulky combat gear but...

"You're... a woman?" he blurted.

Darya raised an eyebrow. "Why? You have a problem with strong women, *malen'kiy*? Or maybe you've not learned how to talk to one yet? Are you nervous? A virgin, perhaps? Get over it, we're just like anybody else. Well, maybe not me but, treat us with respect and don't place *your* expectations on *us* and you'll do fine, handsome boy like you."

"Wait, I'm not... I don't—" Royston stuttered.

Darya held up a hand like a shovel. "Enough! Now, if we're to have any chance of killing this thing we need to link up with what's left of my unit."

"You want *me* to join *you?*" Royston blurted.

The orc grinned. "Why not, I need numbers and, at the very least, I'll have time to think of a new plan while it's chewing on your over-long ass."

"Why?" the young knight asked. "Why are you trying to kill it?"

Darya's features became sombre. She looked up into the night sky.

"After we fled the battle, once our senses started to return, we found a massacre. A small cottage in the woods, the family slaughtered. With no orders, nothing better to do, we decided to find whatever committed the deed and put an end to it. We followed it out of Russia, into Kazakhstan, and here we are."

"You never stopped to think you could just run?" Royston asked tentatively.

Darya chuckled, a deep, grating sound.

"Where would we go? We are monsters ourselves. If the Chimaera doesn't kill us, Camelot will.

Either way, maybe we'll get to do some good before we go."

Hearing the sadness in her voice, Royston made a decision.

"Alright, let's go. Once we kill this thing, we'll see what we can do for you."

Darya chuckled again.

"Assuming any of us survive the night, Sir Knight."

The trek back up the river valley would have taken longer, but for the enhanced knight and manipulated orc warrior, it proved to be little hardship. Caution slowed their passage, listening and watching the starlit sky, stepping quietly and skirting patches of scree to avoid betraying their position.

More than once Darya froze and Royston thought he smelled the chemical carrion stench of their quarry on the wind, and each time he had to try and assure himself that it was *them* doing the hunting, not the twisted beast that stalked these hills.

Leading the way into a shallow gully, the orc held up a hand.

"The others are here. Wait here while I explain things to them."

Watching her leave, Royston briefly wondered if this was where the ambush would come.

No, he decided. Darya had had plenty of opportunity to kill him. She could have left him in the river, tossed him back in or overpowered him while he was disoriented. *If* the orc meant to betray him, it would be to use him as bait for the chimaera, but he was willing to give cooperation a try, rather than automatically mistrust her.

"Sir Royston?"

The call was just loud enough to carry to him and, taking a steadying breath, he threw back his shoulders, attempting to carry himself with more confidence and pride than he felt.

No fire burned in the gully. Royston knew orcs were made to be rugged, able to handle extremes of temperature, but the idea of them just sitting in the dark, as sensible as it was with the chimaera hunting them, was more than a little unsettling.

Darya stood, watching him approach and, beyond her, two more of the warped warriors sat, weapons rested on their laps.

"I thought there were six of you?" Royston made it a question.

"That monster killed *Fyodor* while you and Darya were taking your little swim," one of the orcs replied sourly.

"Sir Royston, this is *Marat* and *Sasha*, the last of my unit."

"Uh, hi," the young knight ventured hesitantly.

Four mismatched eyes studied him sceptically.

"So," he cleared his throat nervously, "what's the plan?"

"Damned if I know," Darya shrugged. "Even with the element of surprise we can't even wound the beast, let alone kill it."

Royston rubbed his chin thoughtfully. "Well, what do you know about it?"

"It's one of a series of prototypes," Sasha volunteered. "I heard that the magi who built the dragon combined different elements in stages. The goal for this creature was something that could fly and spit fire. That's why the extra heads, see? To manage the extra abilities of flight and fire. Of course, since the programme was overseen by that mad bitch Morgana it had to have some significance, so it became a Chimaera."

"It's not just that," Marat rumbled in reply. "I had guard duty at the genetics facility for a while, before they turned me into this. Morgana decided to improve the Chimaera, by adding the Nemean Lion into the mix. You know that one, Sir Knight?" the orc used the title scathingly. "A beast whose hide cannot be pierced by any weapon. She was obsessed with myths and legends, trying to bring back a time that never even existed, of gods and monsters; fucking insanity."

Royston ignored the barb.

"Just another step of the process, perhaps," he replied evenly. "We fired tanks at the dragon, we couldn't scratch it. I'm guessing this animal has a similar augmentation, or spell, woven into the mix. What else do you know about it?"

"We know it can't truly fly. Its wings only allow it to make short assisted jumps, a few hundred metres at best," Darya supplied.

"And its senses are sharp, far keener than ours. I'm starting to think it knew we were waiting for it every time. The lion head spits fire, the goat acid, the snake head is either poisonous, caustic or both, I'm not sure, we never had time to stop and study the effects.”

Royston nodded, “What about behaviour? There are several towns further upriver on the tributaries. Do you think it will go after them?”

Marat shook his head. “No, it’s chased us ever since we tried to kill it at the farm. This thing, I think it feels we challenged it, and it won’t let that rest. The only reason it hasn’t wiped us out already is that it’s playing with us, killing us one at a time. Maybe you now, too,” the gruff orc gestured at Royston.

“We planned to try attacking while it was eating Katya. It just came down out of the night, landed on her and took her away. There was nothing we could do,” Sasha spoke, voice full of regret.

“That was when you showed up,” Marat went on. “When it tossed you and Darya into the river we thought we had it cornered, so we pressed our attack. That’s when it killed Fyodor.”

“So, what weapons do we have?” Royston was thinking fast. This thing might know where they were even now. Speed was of the essence and, if the orcs were right, there was no point laying an ambush, but they didn’t mean they couldn’t set a trap.

“Limited ammunition, a few thirty millimetre grenades. But they did no more to it than the bullets, maybe disoriented it momentarily,” Sasha shrugged.

“Tell me this, when you attacked it before, did you use standard tactics?” Royston asked.

Darya was watching him intently. “It was a lone target. We set an arc of fire where we wouldn’t risk hitting each other and gave it all we had. Overwhelm with concentrated fire, it's how we were trained."

"But, you were all in front of it, yes?" The young knight was getting animated now.

"Yes," Darya confirmed.

"Then we need to split its concentration. There's four of us, and it only has three heads, we surround it, draw each head in a different direction."

"To what end?" Marat rumbled. The big orc seemed unconvinced.

"Well," Royston tried to sound confident, "I noticed that the dragon didn't ignite all the fuel for its fire. The system worked, but it wasn't totally refined. I figure that, being a prototype, there might be a weakness in the fuel delivery system for the fire breath. If we can trigger a flashback, we can kill this thing, or grievously wound it, enough to kill it with conventional means."

"What would you know of Morgana's dragon *malen'kiy?*" Marat chuckled nastily.

Royston blinked. "I was there, I fought it. I was there when it was killed."

Darya raised her eyebrows in surprise. Marat grumbled but said nothing.

"And how do we trigger this flashback?" Sasha asked.

"Well, I've got my arrows, but I lost my bow." Royston thought for a moment, then pointed. "Those thirty millimetre grenades, mounted on spears. Shove one of them down its throat."

Darya scratched her huge square jaw.

"While it spits fire, and tries to kill us?" she rumbled.

Royston shrugged, apologetically, "I mean, if any of you have any better ideas?"

Darya shared a dubious look with Sasha, then looked to the sulking Marat who raised his head.

"Fuck it, it's not like we have anything better to do tonight," he spat.

"But how do we bring it to us?" Darya asked.

"We don't," Royston replied.

A monstrous bellow reverberated through the river valley. All four of them turned to watch the sky, listening to the dying echoes all around them.

Royston swallowed, "We're going to it."

An hour of preparation, and the group was ready to move.

In the small hours of the morning, the stars glittered overhead.

The valley walls on either side of this stretch of the Tente River rose sharply, scattered with small, dense growths of pine, evergreen fingers reaching for the sky.

Despite being sure the Chimaera would know when they approached, Royston and his new comrades moved with as much stealth as they could. They wanted the beast to feel confident in its superiority, rather than have it suspect a change in their behaviour.

Stopping intermittently, Royston swept the landscape with his ocular implant. He regretted the loss of his helmet and was starting to appreciate the shortcomings of his augmentations. The systems in his helmet might not have the acuity of his implant, but that very sharpness of focus dialled his perception down to a point. A fine thing once he had a clear target, not so great for sweeping a landscape to acquire one. Unable to repair the advanced armour, they'd cannibalised several components for their preparations, crafting crude trigger mechanisms from springs and pins taken from the helm and the salvaged weapons of the orcs' fallen comrades.

Still, they were headed to the site of the last contact. After speaking with Darya, Royston concluded that the beast was conditioned in the malice typical of Morgana's creations. Since the initial confrontation at the farm, it had taken only one member of the orc unit at a time, leaving the rest to stew in their loss and sense of powerlessness. Using that framework, and taking its evidently sharp senses into account, Royston reasoned that it was unlikely to waste energy roaming these hills until it was ready to attack, or until it had finished its latest meal.

Creeping through the night, wincing at every crack of a twig, or shift of stone underfoot, they made the best time they could to the clearing. Taking care to circle and approach from downwind, they all picked up the charnel stench of the creature before they even spotted it, cutting through the strong pine scent of the trees.

In the time since they left the gully, Royston had managed to convince himself he was wrong, that there was no chance the beast would be where they left it. But, despite the certainty he had nurtured in the course of their approach, there it was. The hulking, ragged mongrel, a twisted product of tainted science and corrupt magic lay, its forepaws clutching the masticated remains of two orcs, a bloody pile of ragged meat and jumbled bones.

Unable to prepare the site of their attack, Royston's meagre cohort had made the best of what equipment they had left between them. Aside from the main plan, Royston drew on his experience with the dragon, and the first objective in both cases was to keep the thing on the ground.

With the target in sight, the plan went into action.

When they'd faced the dragon, Royston and his comrades had still been relatively green. Warriors of skill, certainly, but not really a cohesive unit. In the orcs, Royston had a group who were used to working together, skilled and seasoned soldiers, now without the unfortunate element of drug-induced berserker rage.

At his signal, they split, melting into the shadows of the trees.

Holding his position, Royston watched, seeking the subtle signs that the Chimaera had detected them. Both lion and goat heads gnawed upon the bones before it, the one down, fangs flashing and grinding, whiskers bristling, the other raised, a femur nestled in its curiously animated lips, tongue seeking stray morsels, horizontal pupils staring seemingly at nothing as it sucked the marrow. The snake head lolled, coiled on the creature's haunches.

The lion paused in its feeding, ears twitching. Its nostrils let out a loud 'huff' of breath.

This was the first signal. With Darya and Marat on either side, Sasha had just moved downwind, announcing their presence without a doubt.

Now for the surprise.

Marshalling his courage, Royston leapt from cover with a bellowed challenge that sounded thin and reedy to his own ears.

The Chimaera turned, blinking in feline surprise, lips drawing back in a snarl of anticipation, but Royston was already casting the first of his spears. Little more than a bomb on a stick, he threw the shaft, mounted with one of their few grenades, to land at the feet of the monster. By some miracle the trigger worked, and the Chimaera was engulfed in fire, noise and dust. The sound of the explosion echoed off the walls of the valley but, even as the first report came back, the beast expelled the dust and smoke with a fierce sweep of its wings; the second signal.

Springing from their own concealment, Darya and Marat advanced swinging bolas above their heads. The Chimaera paused, its goat and snake heads fixing these new targets as its wings furled ever so slightly. Seeing their chance, both orcs threw.

Fashioned from gun slings and river rocks, the bolas arced out, wrapping each of the giant bat wings, looping and lacing around themselves to bind them in place. Hefting their spears, Royston and the orcs advanced, circling, passing from one head's field of vision to the next. The Chimaera hunkered down, snarling, bleating and hissing, swinging its heads to follow the prey.

Darting in, Royston lunged, his second spear tip fended away by a swipe of a mangy paw, the sharp edge of torn plate steel glancing across the impervious hide. Taking his lead, Darya and Marat started to goad the creature too, striking and withdrawing, staying out of easy reach. The Chimaera snarled, trying to lunge in one, then two directions at once, hobbling itself with split decision.

Sensing the monster's rising frustration, Royston gave a whistle and Sasha emerged from the bushes to join the dance. Spears jabbed toward its eyes, ears and underside, scraped across its flanks as the Chimaera sought to coordinate itself. It spat acid at Darya, the goat's aim thrown off as the snake head lunged at Sasha, only to be denied as the lion recoiled from Royston's thrust and aggravated more as Marat's spear dragged across its ribs.

Deciding to seek the advantage, the Chimaera flexed its powerful wings, only to discover that the improvised bolas' straps had been laced with pieces of armour-grade steel, shorn from the orcs' improvised maille. The splinters slashed into the soft, leather hide of the wing membranes, shredding and slicing. With a snap, the straps burst apart, but the result of the ensuing beat only succeeded in throwing the confused Chimaera off-balance, allowing the warriors around it to renew their assault.

Reaching a momentary consensus, the creature wheeled on Marat, lion's head drawing a deep breath, preparing to spit all-consuming fire at its tormentor.

"Now!" Royston yelled.

Tossing the spear into a throwing grip, Marat heaved as the Chimaera lunged forward.

The aim was true. Royston could see it as his implant enhanced his neurochemistry, tracking and predicting the weapon's arc. The spear would enter the monster's mouth just as planned, unless...

The Chimaera's reflexes were sharper than they'd expected.

With a conceited twist of its head, the beast tossed the spear aside at the last second, the weapon clattering to the copse floor undetonated. Royston experienced a split-second of shock before a bright wave of heat washed out from the Chimaera's mouth and flames engulfed Marat.

Bellowing like a dying bull, the orc flailed, tossing himself to the floor as the monster whipped around. The goat's head spewed a wide arc of noxious acid that caught a stunned Sasha across the chest, dragging an ululating cry of panic and pain from him. A massive paw struck him from his feet and tossed him back into the trees.

Teeth gritted in grim determination, Darya fought on, jabbing at the writhing snake's head, trading its strikes against her own. Royston dashed across the goat's field of vision, trying to catch its attention, to get the monster back off-balance. The head bleated and he shoved his own spear forward, only to have it deftly caught, the haft snapped in the goat's flat, blood-stained teeth.

Spitting a curse, Royston snatched a glance to Marat's fallen spear, only for a loud scream to drag his eyes back to the scene.

Looped around her waist, the snake lifted Darya, hefting her into the air to land heavily in front of the smiling, salivating lion's mouth. She rolled with the impact, keeping her grip on her spear through sheer stubborn tenacity. As the lion pulled back to strike, Darya seemed to reach a decision. With a swift, brutal movement, she snapped the spear's haft on her knee and thrust the shortened weapon forward as the lion's teeth flashed down.

Fire blossomed, exploding out from the Chimaera's mouth, crawling across the flesh of the lion's head. The monster yowled in pain, tossing its prey aside. Darya screamed and Royston leapt, unthinking, to grab her by her tac-harness, dragging her clear, and noting only peripherally that her arm now ended in a ragged stump.

Getting her into the shadows of the trees, he rested her against a trunk.

Sweat glistened on the grey skin of her forehead, her teeth gritted against the pain. Royston leaned down to inspect the damage, when her other hand shoved him away so hard he stumbled.

"What are you doing? Finish the fight!" she hissed.

Staring stupidly at her, Royston shook himself.

Right, finish the fight.

With a quick nod he turned and leapt back into the clearing, heading straight for the last spear.

The Chimaera rolled around on the ground but the very noxious nature of its fire worked against it, clinging and burning. In a moment of desperation, the goat's head spat, dousing the flames but melting the skin and muscle underneath. Roused to new heights of agony, the beast thrashed in the dirt until, with an almighty roar, it threw itself to its feet, turning toward the last of its foes; Royston.

The shaft of his explosive-tipped weapon firmly in hand, Royston faced the Chimaera. Under the waxing light of dawn the creature took shaking steps, half of its lion's head a bloody ruin, bone peaking through the ravaged flesh. With a roar it made to spit fire, but only managed to spew burning fuel from the ruin of its cheek, the potent accelerant clearly only causing it more pain.

Taking the opportunity Royston skipped forward, thrusting out. The spear entered the cavernous mouth, the point jarring against the bone and muscle within, striking the trigger and... nothing.

The explosive was a dud, or maybe the trigger got damaged. Royston's mind raced as a huge paw descended, swatting him into the trees with all the force of a car-crash. Branches whipped at him, pine needles scratched him until he hit a tree-trunk with a blow that spun him around. He lay, dazed and disoriented on the ground.

A roar and a crash sounded the pursuit of the Chimaera. Obviously it was done with the game and now wished only to see Royston and his comrades dead. Struggling to his feet, the knight staggered away, hoping to lead the monster away from Darya at least.

Bursting from the trees, the Chimaera roared again. Royston ducked the swing of its paw, but the creature span, its thick snake's-head-tail looping under him and throwing him again.

Dashed against a tree, landing with a whiplash impact, the young knight groaned. Rolling over, trying to get hands and feet underneath him, his head spun, his body on fire with every movement even as his hand fell onto a familiar shape.

Struggling to focus, he looked down and...

His bow, right there in his palm as if it had always been there.

The Chimaera, maddened with pain, cannoned through the trees.

Fingers tightening around the grip, Royston rolled, coming to his knees. An arrow already at the knock, he drew, breathed, loosed... and missed.

Vision swimming, he shook his head, throwing himself clumsily aside as the monster came for him once more. The beast leapt, bowling the disoriented knight from his feet, bearing him to the ground and landing astride him. It reached for him with the lion's mouth, but Royston shoved a gauntleted hand out, clawing at the exposed eye socket on the ruined half of its face. With a cry of pain, the lion withdrew, the goat assuming its place, jaw grinding as if it was chewing cud, not preparing to douse him with acid.

Scrabbling at his quiver, Royston dragged an arrow out and jabbed at the goat's eye, sinking the shaft into the fluid-filled sack. Upon impact, the flechette arrow disbursed a bundle of monofilament wire on a tiny gas explosive charge, the wire whipping and expanding like a nest of snakes made from piano-wire.

The goat bleated in distress and the Chimaera staggered. Royston rolled up once again, another arrow in his hand, his delicate optic augmentation swinging out, accounting for his dizziness as he drew the shaft.

The lion whipped around, lunging again and Royston, mind clear, let fly.

The armour-piercing depleted-uranium loaded broadhead struck the exposed eye-socket of the lion's head, smashing into the delicate bone there, punching through flesh, bone, brain-matter, and out the creature's skull like a grotesque flower in bloom.

The weight of the dying creature rolled over the knight, catching him up as the two rolled down the steep valley side, coming eventually to rest in a tangle of limbs and broken boughs.

Royston opened his eyes, he tasted blood on his lips and every part of him ached. The Chimaera's massive foreleg held him in a death's embrace. He could feel it's lagging heart beating out its last, but he was almost certain it was done for. With a deep sigh of relief, tinged with pain, he closed his eyes for a moment.

His ears detected the rustling, but his mind assumed it must be a survivor, Darya or Sasha, coming to find him. Then he felt the muscles beneath him shift and heard a deep hiss.

His eyes flashed open as the snake struck, and a deafening sound left his ears ringing.

The snake head flopped limp, a large-calibre hole punched through the roof of its mouth, daylight visible through the hole in its head.

Twisting awkwardly, Royston turned, staring down the barrel of a massive pistol, straight into the eyes of Commander Altynai Ospanova, sitting somewhat uncomfortably astride Artemis.

Relief flooded his body like a cooling salve, his hurts mattering less and less now help was here. A half hysterical cry slipped from his cracked and bloodied lips.

"What times are these," she said, affecting a tone of wonderment, "when the damsel comes to the knight's rescue?"

Coming Soon from David Cartwright:

Chapter 1

London crawled past the limousine windows. Many things had changed in the time since the le Fay campaign, Rosalyn Pendragon (Taunton-Savant in public), Knight of Essex mused, but nothing short of a blanket artillery barrage could help London traffic.

The Round Table of Camelot had seen more than half its seats vacated by traitors and casualties to the onset of the conflict. Over time some had been elevated to fill the seats, more lost to the fighting. Still, with the war fought and won, the Table was returning to full strength, although the number of actual knights was still much reduced.

Camelot had long held to the values of peace and understanding, Ros contemplated. There had been enough violence at its birth to ensure that Camelot disdained wars fought for power or profit. It would have been easy for a small, fledgling nation, bound to a small island, to let itself become arrogant or avaricious. To push out, fighting for fortune or conquest. But, under the leadership of the line of Pendragon, the Table only unsheathed its steel in defence of those who found themselves under threat from such unwanted attentions.

The history of Europe had, undoubtedly, been a tumultuous one, but the nations had come into concert since the last Great War. Although, having now fought one, Rosalyn disdained the term. But, it was the wider world that now concerned the throne.

Russia had been a veiled nation under Morgana, the secret seat of her power until it rose like an angry bear to maul Camelot, driven by the sorceress queen's thirst for vengeance.

Relations with the Middle East and the Southern Asian continent were similarly shadowed, not obscured entirely, but murky to say the least.

Regions of Africa were still alight with inter-nation warfare. Prior to the outbreak of war in Europe, service to the friendly governments of the continent were a sure way to win honour and station for a knight of the Table.

The Americas were almost entirely unknown, and apparently content to stay that way. What little the agents of Camelot had gleaned from talks with the Inuit tribes of Greenland (or Avalon, as it had been known) spoke of peoples and Nations with unfamiliar practices and unexplored technologies which might bring untold benefit, *if* the appropriate political inroads could be made. If anything the le Fay war had made that less likely.

Still, rumours were surfacing, strange and disquieting reports from all quarters. Unexplained events and unprecedented encounters. Rosalyn and her comrades had learned, during the conflict, that the magic so inherently tied to the myth of Camelot, the magic that had been so thoroughly sanitised from the great edifice of history, was real and always had been.

Morgana le Fay had banked on it, distilled and hoarded it for her own use but, in the end, it had been released, diffused into the atmosphere and the fabric of the world. Ever since that day, strange things had started to occur.

Ros watched the buildings out of the window, smoothing the creases of her maroon suit pants and stretching out her long legs. Even she had to admit they were long. As part of her post-knighthood genetic and bionic enhancement, she was now seven-foot-six and capable of tossing a small car, even without her power-assisted armour. She'd surpassed the estimate for her final height by two clear inches after the recent round of treatments. It was strange to think that the whole process started as little as eighteen months before.

The car rolled slowly down Tottenham Court Road, Centre Point looming large ahead, on approach to Castle Camelot. The first shudder of the earth passed with little notice, but the second caused the six-ton armoured luxury car and its two-hundred and sixty pound occupant to jump from the road, landing with a heavy jolt back on the tarmac.

Skidding to a halt amid a knot of cars, drivers leaning on their horns either in confusion or from being knocked senseless, the limousine idled for a moment before being tossed in the air once more.

Arms outstretched to brace for the impact, Rosalyn snarled an oath and, as the suspension struggled to cushion their descent, she popped the door open and emerged onto the panicked street.

Chunks of concrete rained from the grey tower of Centre Point as the tower block shivered. Augmented eyes peering through the rising dust, Rosalyn could make out no sign of the attackers, no weapons' vapour trails, no smoke from explosions.

Even as she watched, the earth beneath the tower started to bulge, stone, steel and tarmac screeching in protest, alongside the running people, screaming in fear and confusion. Rosalyn leapt into action, intent on lending what aid she could, either by evacuating the building or clearing the injured to a safe distance. But, with a final despairing crack and groan, the tower shattered. Rubble rained down, like sand into the bottom of an egg-timer. A billow of dust blasted out to engulf the surrounding streets, propelled along the lip of the cacophonous roar of the dying building.

Consumed by the cloud, it was as if night fell upon Rosalyn, the sun blotted out to a dim glow, all sound suddenly muffled. If not for sound-dampening augmentations in her ears, they would surely be ringing now.

Half blind and coughing from the dust she pressed on, pulling her pocket square and pressing it over her mouth and nose. There were still screams ahead, survivors and victims of this... this what?

What was going on?

The press of retreating civilians surged around her, pushing her back despite her immense strength. The peal of sirens cut through the dust-laden air, though only seconds had passed. Ros found herself at the lip of the collapse, rubble and vehicles intertwined amid the ruin. On the ground before her a woman knelt beside a man, partially pinned under a shifted car.

Crouching, Ros placed a hand on the woman's shoulder. Bemused, tear-streaked eyes turned to her from a dusk-caked face.

"Can you hear me?" Ros asked, voice terse.

The woman frowned in confusion.

Quickly, Ros assessed the state of the injured man then took the woman's hands, placed them on his lapels and mimed jerking motions until the stricken woman nodded in understanding. Taking up station beside the car Ros bent her legs, gripped the chassis and heaved. Metal and rubble shifted as the car raised, the woman dragging the injured man away. Dropping the car, Ros beckoned her to keep on to the pavement and glanced around, looking for the next victim.

A slide of rubble from above and a dull rumble was all the warning she got before *something* raised itself from beneath the heap-that-was Centre Point.

A great spine, shedding chunks of debris, each disc bigger than a truck tyre arched upward, lifting a massive skull atop its length. Ribs, shoulder blades, clavicle, bones formed from the swirling cloud of mist, like swarms of flies under some obscene influence, coalescing from the air. Even as Ros watched in growing horror, glistening meat crawled across the towering skeleton. The arms, unfinished as they were, extended skyward in a pose of victory. Organs, muscle and sinew, great lungs inflated like bellows as the molten, steaming flesh rolled into place. The throat let out a wet exaltation until there was tongue and lips to form it into words.

"Ow dhewheles ov vyth!" the giant thundered, for that was all Ros could name the creature.

Eighty feet tall by Rosalyn's guess, the great figure swung its head to left and right, taking in the buildings that surrounded it.

"Wait, Cornish?" Rosalyn blinked as the giant lifted first one, then another foot from the rubble-pile.

It came as some relief when, whatever power had reconstituted this gigantic, and clearly male, figure sent a huge pelt crawling over its body, set with a desiccated mammoth's head as a cod piece.

"Rag henna! Hemm yw Troia Nova!"

"—No, sir! New Troy is long gone, this is London!—" Rosalyn called back, her polyglot implant instantly translating her words.

The giant glanced down at her, a quizzical look about its huge features.

"—Now, as a representative of the civic authorities I must demand—" she began, but whatever scrap of the giant's attention she had held was wrested back.

"Gone!" the giant bellowed. "Corineus had promised my bones to Brutus, a strong foundation for his new settlement. And none stronger than the bones of Gogmagog I'd wager! What folly of mortals allowed it to fall?"

Still bellowing Cornish, the giant allowed its gaze to drop once more to Rosalyn's meagre stature.

Keep it talking, Ros thought to herself. *While it's talking it's not smashing the city.*

"The shadow of the eagle fell across it. The armies of Rome," she explained.

Gogmagog looked about to fly into a rage but Ros kept on with her explanation.

"They themselves have fallen before the blades of the Visigoths. You've been gone a long time Gogmagog, the people around you now are descendants of the Normans, the Saxons and Angles."

"Huh?" the giant seemed unimpressed. "Not a fierce Pict warrior among you? Then I shall raze your settlement, and bring forth my brethren from the ground in which they lay. Corineus and Brutus shall not be the last word in the story of the giants of Albion!"

The last was bellowed at such volume nearby windows shattered under the force.

"I will not allow that!" Rosalyn roared in challenge.

"I may be no Pict, but I am a knight of Camelot, and I shall not see you bring harm to this city!"

"Hah!" Gogmagog let out a bark of joyous laughter.

"Some spirit you have, let us test it!" and, with a sweep of his huge foot, the giant sent Ros, along with a slew of rubble, flying back down the street and into the window screen of her own limo. The inch-thick blast-proof laminate glass spider-webbed as she hit with a sound like a gunshot, sagging and cushioning some of the blow. Still, Ros felt she could hear her reinforced skeleton groan under the impact.

Starting from the roadside, her driver, interrupted from setting up an impromptu triage, took two steps toward her until she shot him a fierce glare. With a grimace, she hauled herself from the smashed windscreen, shaking fragments of glass from her clothing.

"That about does it for this suit," she lamented, reaching into the driver's footwall to trigger the release catch on the car's luggage compartment.

"It couldn't end with dragons and sorcerers, vampires and monsters, oh no!" she grumbled under her breath. Circling to the rear of the car she reached down, retrieving her badge of office, the sword of the House of Essex.

Grim-faced, she drew the blade, tossing the scabbard back into the car and striding back the way Gogmagog had so casually tossed her.

"Hear me, Gogmagog!" she roared in challenge.

The giant was peering playfully in nearby windows, delighting in tormenting those trapped within. He ignored her completely.

Without breaking stride, Rosalyn scooped a chunk of concrete, all twenty kilos of it, from the ground and hefted it to her shoulder before shot-putting it at Gogmagog. The concrete exploded against the back of the giant's head.

Bull's-eye from sixty yards, not bad, Ros thought to herself as the giant turned, murder in his eyes.

"I am Rosalyn, of the House of Essex, Knight of the Round Table, death of the witch Morgana le Fay and Dragon slayer! Cease your hostility against this city and come quietly. I do not have time for your shit!"

The giant, eyes alight with amusement, burst into full-throated laughter.

"Some claim! If you can lend to your arm the strength of your boasts, this will be a fine match!"

Reaching down, the giant pulled an I-beam from the rubble, hefting a ton of steel as if it were a birch switch.

Ros ground her teeth in frustration and thumbed the control ring set just beneath the pommel of her sword. The blade lit up with actinic fire as the power systems installed within sprang to life.

Gogmagog's grin faded.

"Witchcraft!" the giant spat, voice dripping malice.

Rosalyn levelled the blade at the giant's chest.

"Don't make me kill you, Gogmagog."

With a mighty roar the Giant swung his improvised club, kicking up dust and scattering rubble and fragments of glass. Ros gripped her sword hilt, lunging low as her spitting blade carved the onrushing steel like a Sunday roast as it passed over her head. Standing and spinning she brought her weapon down, finishing the cut and, as Gogmagog raised the I-beam again, a length fully four feet long dropped to the tarmac with a 'clang!'

As the echoes died, Ros shouted, "Cease this, or I'll chop off your manhood next!"

Drawing his lips back in a feral snarl, the giant raised the club high, bringing it straight down toward Ros who, thinking the blow strangely clumsy, side-stepped easily.

The truth of the giant's goal was revealed a split-second later when the blow raised another cloud of dust, obscuring Rosalyn's vision. Only her enhanced reflexes saved her as, through the new cloud, the great club scythed, its tip drawing a line of sparks as it scraped along the tarmac. Without her augmentations, Ros might have been dashed to pieces by the feint and furious attack. As it was she barely brought her sword up, only to be caught up on the beam as it swung. Her arms absorbed most of the blow but her sword bit deep and stuck. A split-second's reflex saw Ros clinging to the I-beam as it reached the apex and end of its arc.

Gogmagog raised a hand to shield his eyes from the sun, staring off, club raised, into the distance.

"Huh," he chuckled, "good swing. Can't even see where she went."

With a fierce scowl set to her features, Ros launched herself from the steel beam, bringing both hands together and forcing power through her servo-assisted joints to land a powerful blow to the back of the giant's neck.

Gogmagog staggered, giving Ros a moment to seat herself astride his shoulders. As he straightened, she delivered a ringing hammer-blow to the bone behind the giant's ear. Reaching around, she grabbed handfuls of the giant's scraggly beard, locking her legs and ankles into a stranglehold around his neck, the muscles in her legs coming alight as she squeezed.

Gasping, the giant swatted at the back of his neck with an open palm, a concussion that would have killed an unaugmented human. Without her armour, Ros felt her ears pop and her ribs creak but she held fast. The huge hand came back in an attempt to pry her loose but, releasing the beard and arching her spine, Ros leaned back, caught the giant's little finger and, with a savage twist of her body, dislocated the oversized digit. As the hand withdrew, Ros sat bolt upright, this time swinging a high blow to the giant's temple before focussing on squeezing the breath from the monster.

Staggering, gasping and spinning, Gogmagog slammed into one building, then another. Glass showered around Ros until, disoriented, the giant stumbled across Tottenham Court Tube Station, tripping over the shiny steel box. With a deafening crash, Gogmagog sprawled face down onto the road, spilling Ros to tumble away.

Lying on her back, breathing heavily, Ros grinned, alive and victorious, the giant huffing powerful breaths nearby.

The ground shuddered.

Rolling her head, Ros turned to see Gogmagog plant a fist against the tarmac, straining to rise once more.

With a pained grimace, Rosalyn willed herself to roll to her feet, numerous scrapes and budding bruises voicing their complaints at this irrational action.

The giant got one fist in place, then planted another, heaving himself to all fours.

Willing one foot to follow another, Rosalyn staggered to where the giant's fallen club lay, the sword of Essex still embedded and flashing like a magnesium flare. Heedless of the grunts from her opponent, Ros reached down, gripping the cold steel and hauling one end, wrapping both arms around it. Sensing rather than seeing Gogmagog raise his head, Rosalyn heaved the I-beam around in a slow but inexorable circle, the end lifting as the beam moved faster and faster.

Ros's eyes locked with Gogmagog's in the moment before the beam struck home.

Not given to flights of fancy, Ros couldn't shake the idea that there was a look of strange satisfaction, approval even, in the giant's eye as a ton of steel clanged against the side of his head, carrying him off his hands and sending him, pole-axed, back to the ground.

Ros stood for a moment, chest heaving before dropping the massive weight of the beam. With a shaking hand, she retrieved her sword and, after a moment watching Gogmagog's chest rise and fall, she thumbed the control ring to deactivate the blade.

Sirens and lights arrived at the scene, accompanied by armoured, mounted knights. At their head, Dame Seraphine Feldon sat ramrod straight atop her fourth gen C.T.E.E.D.

Reined in, the cybernetic stallion pawed at the ground as Seraphine took in the scene.

Wearily Rosalyn rose from the pavement and went to brief her mentor.

"Ma'am," she greeted her. "My driver has a triage station set up about a hundred yards back up Tottenham Court, I got city to shut down power and gas lines into this zone, and I've apprehended the culprit."

She waved a hand toward the recumbent figure of Gogmagog.

"You might want to call in a flatbed or something..." she tailed off.

Seraphine's cool blue eyes showed no sign of surprise, or anything else which might betray if this unprecedented event had ruffled her composure.

"Rosalyn," she replied finally. "You've been a knight for over a year, you can call me 'Seraphine' you know. Now go and see a medic. That's an order."

Camelot 2052: Old New Worlds